CHILDREN
of
YRATHEA

To you.

CONTENTS

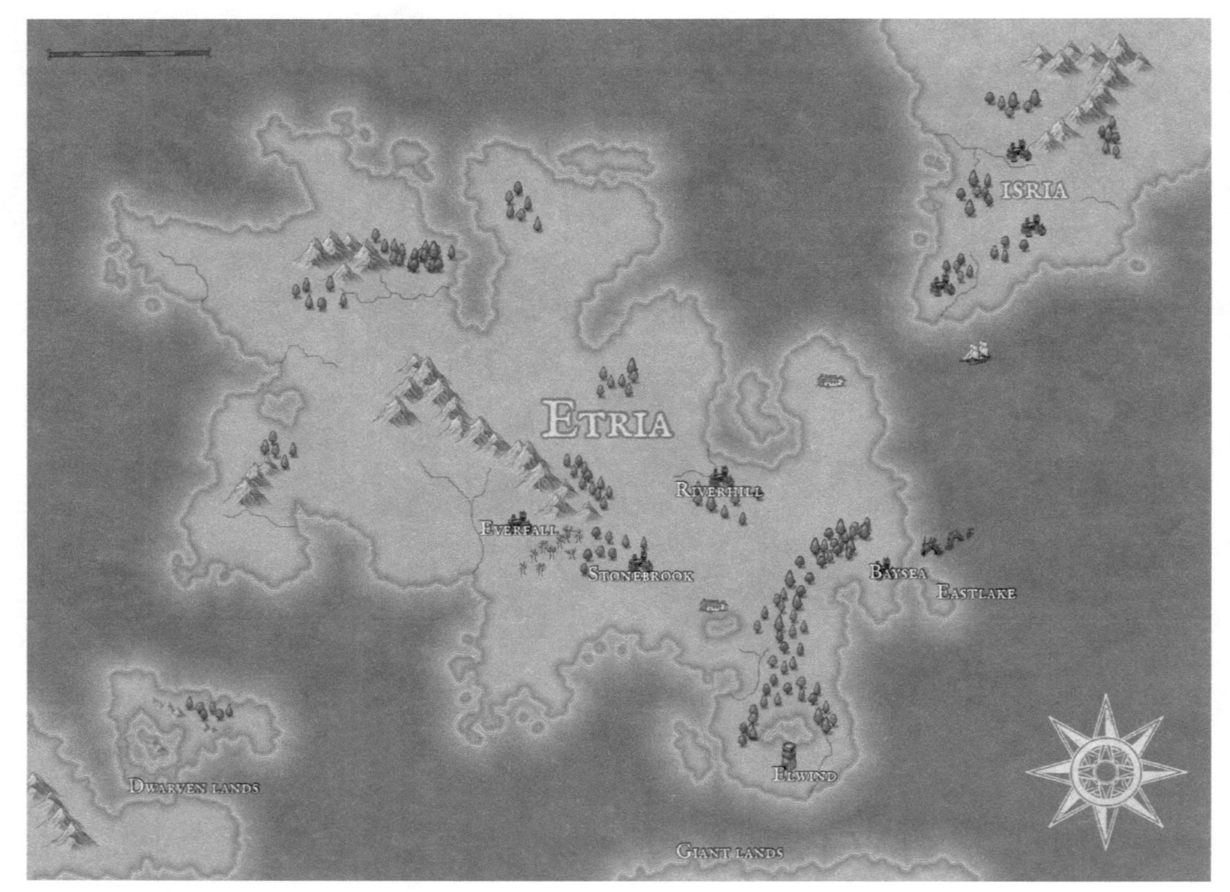

ISRIA
ETRIA
RIVERHILL
EVERFALL
STONEBROOK
BAYSEA
EASTLAKE
ELWIND
DWARVEN LANDS
GIANT LANDS

I

DREAD

That year, the Festival of Life would end early.

The city of Eastlake was up bright and early for the festivities. It had been decorated with vibrant colors, in sashes and flowers spread throughout the streets. Stalls were opened in the square, offering treats you could only find during the occasion along with all the products the city was known for. And right in the middle a large stage stood, as colorful as everything around it, waiting for the presentation to start.

Beside the stage, a tent had been reserved for the dancers about to perform.

"How do you know the flowers aren't all going to fall off while you're dancing?" a blonde girl asked as her cousin examined herself in the mirror.

"You just have to tie them properly, it's not hard. I'll teach you before your turn next year," the young woman, Teiwa, grinned at the girl and turned back to the mirror to tie another flower in her auburn hair. She pulled a loose strand and tied it behind a long, pointed ear, then gave it a slight tug. Satisfied, she nodded to herself.

"Who says I'm going to dance next year?" The girl, Kadi, made a comically exaggerated face of disgust.

"Tradition, I guess." She shrugged, took another flower from the basket and stared at it longingly. "I don't know what it is, but I feel... Weird."

The younger of the two rolled her eyes. "You are weird. Maybe not that type of weird, but weird."

The young woman turned to look at her, an amused expression on her face. "Aren't you supposed to be elsewhere? Watching the twins or something?"

"Nah." Kadi shrugged. "Mama's got them."

"I thought Auntie was watching a stall."

"This is your first year dancing with the adults, so she asked someone to take care of it for her so she could watch. Besides, there's barely any customers anyway, just about everyone's out by the stage."

The red haired woman dropped the flower in her hand. She'd turned twenty that spring, making her officially an adult. While there was no coming of age ceremony during the festival, for a young woman, the first year dancing amongst the adults was just as good. To know hers was going to be watched by such a large crowd put a weight in her stomach.

"Everyone?"

"I know, it's weird! The dances are always a success, but not this much. Anyway, we got spots right at the front to watch you! The whole family will be there."

"So no pressure, right?"

"Right," the girl grinned. "Good luck."

The young woman watched as her cousin ran out of the tent to join the rest of their family. On the other side, the other women chatted amongst themselves, casting her a glance now and then. When she looked their way, they stopped immediately. She sighed. Though she was used to it by now, it would never cease to bother her.

The crowd watched with excitement as the music stopped and the group of women climbed the stairs onto the stage, their skirts as bright and vivid as the decoration around them, and their hair adorned with flowers of all sorts. One by one, they took their place on stage.

"You got this, Tei, honey!" someone called from the spectators.

"Yeah, kick their ass!" someone else added, certainly her cousin Kadi. Teiwa could almost see her being scolded for her language.

The other women giggled.

Teiwa groaned. Her aunt had probably had the best intentions in mind, but her cousin must be loving the opportunity to mess with her. She took a deep breath and assumed the starting pose for the dance.

As the music started, all young women dove forward into the stage, passing by each other in graceful movements as they changed formations over and over. The crowd clapped in rhythm with the song. Then, in perfect sync, half the women pulled sashes from within their blouses and tossed one end to the other half. They proceeded to continue their dance, now forming braids with their sashes as they moved past one another. Teiwa focused and tried hard not to get any movements wrong. There was no punishment for messing up, at least not officially, but she was not about to add "ruined the festival dance" to her list of reasons to be singled out.

Off to the side, the drums began a heavier beat. All women ran to one corner of the stage, where they dropped the sashes and took hold of a much larger fabric, dyed a crimson red. They ran back into position and lowered it to the floor. Then, right as the drums beat harder, they raised it fast. Again they lowered it and raised, following the beat. Teiwa watched the underside of the fabric as it flew up, creating a space under it where soon they would take turns crossing, paying attention to get her turn right. As the fabric moved past her face on the third time, however, there was a man standing right before her.

His skin was pale and there were stains all over his face and clothes. He opened his mouth, his expression that of pure agony, and blood dripped from it as he reached out for her.

She fell to the ground screaming.

The others dropped the fabric and rushed to her side, and as it fell, it lay perfectly flat on the floor.

All around her was a cacophony of sounds as the young women tried to ask if she was in pain and the crowd chatted amongst themselves in confusion, trying to understand what had happened. She could only point forward, hand shaking and eyes watery.

"T-the man," she struggled to speak. "There was a man."

The women exchanged confused glances. Some of them rolled their eyes or shook their heads. Then, as they helped Teiwa stand, someone screamed elsewhere.

At the far end of the crowd, people parted as if to make way for something. Shrieks and terrified chatter filled everyone's ears. Teiwa took a tentative step forward, then another. She jumped off the stage as more and more people parted. Now that she was close to them, she could tell they weren't making way, but rather trying to avoid something. She continued moving towards it until the last people moved out of her path.

The man she'd just seen stood there, covered in red stains and reaching for her. As he opened his mouth to speak, blood dripped.

"Help me," he called, crying.

Everything went dark.

When Teiwa woke up, she was in a familiar room. Not her own, but one at the local hospital. She'd been there many times before, visiting her mother at her work. It was also where she'd met one of her two best friends, she recalled, but pushed the thought away from her mind as soon as it came. Her mother sat beside her on the bed, stroking her hair.

"A'mma," she called weakly.

"I'm here, my treasure. You're safe."

"A'mma, there was a man," she continued, sitting up. Her mother slid a hand onto her back to help. "The blood... What happened? Where is he?"

Her mother lowered her eyes. "I'm sorry, my love, he did not make it. We did all we could, I did all I could, but his insides, they..." She shook her head. "No, that's not something you ought to be concerned with."

Teiwa stared at her in horror. What about his insides? With how he looked on the outside, she could only imagine it had been serious, perhaps a fall. But if he'd been in such a terrible accident, would he have been able to walk and speak like that? And where would he even have fallen from to cause such damage?

"Before, I..." she began, hesitant. "I saw him, A'mma. He was on the stage, right in front of me. It was only a moment, but I'm certain it was him."

Her mother looked up at her with a concerned expression. "Are you certain you're not misremembering? The trauma, I'm sure it—"

"I'm not! I know what I saw. He was there, and next thing I know people were screaming in the back where he stumbled in," she said.

"Well, you did seem very frightened over something." Her mother nodded. She touched her daughter's cheek gently and smiled, if only a little. "My treasure, I've always known you were special. Perhaps the gods have sent you a message. But there is nothing to be done now, so try to get some rest." She planted a kiss on her daughter's forehead.

Before Teiwa could speak, her mother stood and left the room. She watched, frustrated. How was she to rest? Her head was spinning with all that happened.

On one hand, she knew this would make her reputation as the odd one even worse. She'd been singled out her whole life, for the shape of her ears, for being the chief's daughter, for being the strange kid who talks to the trees. Nothing she did to fit in seemed to be enough, and now she also got to be the one who screamed and ruined the dance at the festival, on her very first year participating with the adults.

On the other hand, a man was dead. She felt horrible to even worry about her reputation at such a moment. She did not know or understand what could have possibly caused his death, or what her mother meant with what little information she shared about his state, but she couldn't wipe the image of his face from her mind. He was so pale, so devoid of life even as he moved and spoke to her. His eyes were sunken and it was as if, somehow, he was already gone before his body caught up.

She fell back on her pillow and let out a deep sigh.

⁂

"What do you think she saw that made her scream like that?" one of the young women in the hallway asked.

"Probably Ula's ugly face," another replied, laughing.

"Who says she saw anything? She's weird, who's to say she didn't scream just because?" a third one added.

The fourth young woman just nodded along with the others, but said nothing. When they looked at her, she laughed and agreed.

"Have you girls nothing better to do? Surely I can speak to your professors and arrange for a more fitting schedule, if you have so much free time," Ashtari added as she left Teiwa's room.

The young women all froze in place.

"My lady, it's not... We didn't..."

"No, it's not, and you didn't, I'm certain. Now, find something useful to make of yourselves, yes? I will not have you speaking ill of a patient in this hospital, whether they are my family or not, and certainly not while standing right outside their door." She glared at the women through her bright, blue eyes. They squirmed.

"Yes, my lady," one of them was able to get out and the others agreed. Three of them curtsied and left. The last one stood there, head down in shame. Ashtari watched her for a moment and sighed.

"I know peer pressure is hard, and I'm not asking you to be friends with my daughter if you do not wish to, but I expected better of you," she said.

The young woman looked like she might cry. Ashtari watched her for a moment, debating on how to proceed. That attitude had been reprehensible, but she did understand wanting to earn the respect of one's peers. When she came to the island, decades ago, it was not her narrow eyes or her dark hair that gathered unwanted attention. You could find those easily on the streets. No, it was her long ears, with their inward curve from the middle, going back out at the tip, that set her apart. It was a mark of her ancestry, of a people from another country not that far away, but foreign nonetheless. And even though she'd been born in the same nation as every islander around her, was an elf just like every single one of them, it was a clear sign she did not belong. She'd worked hard to earn their respect, force it out of them if needed be. She shouldn't have had to, and she did not wish it upon anyone.

"Come now, how about we check in on the other patients?" She smiled gently and the young woman nodded, head still down and eyes watery. Ashtari laid a hand on her back and guided her down the hallway and into another room.

⁂

"Does it matter, knowing exactly what happened to that man? It will not change his fate," a voice asked gently.

Teiwa shrugged. She was sitting back on a high branch of a tall tree outside her house.

"I just... I want to understand."

A moment passed in silence. Then the voice returned, to Teiwa's ears only.

"I cannot speak for what happened to his insides, as you put it. But I do know what caused it," it said.

Teiwa sat up in a hurry.

"It was a wave of forbidden magic," the tree continued, "and it is fortunate that man was the only person there when it happened, or many more could have died."

She frowned. "Forbidden magic is just a story, it's not real."

"It is very real. It simply had not affected us before. Our mother Yrathea has been absorbing as much of it as she can, protecting us. It appears she can no longer hold it back completely. We are all connected to her, you know that. Us trees more obviously so. I can feel it, the magic running through those connections. It is only a matter of time until it happens again."

Teiwa leaned back against her friend slowly. The ancient tales spoke of a forbidden magic, brought into this world somehow, and how it changed, corrupted everything it touched. Everything, except Yrathea. The sacred tree, the only piece of the Mother Goddess left in this world. She was supposed to withstand anything, so how was it possible that she would be defeated by this magic?

The question didn't leave her mind for the rest of the day. Everywhere she went, people shot her concerned looks, but her mind was too full of thoughts to care. How was she ever to erase the image of that man from her memories? She went to the place he'd come from, where the wave hit. It took a while to convince her friend to tell her where it was, exactly, but she was nothing if not persistent. The grass was dead in an odd, straight line, but nothing else seemed out of the ordinary. For a moment, Teiwa stared at it, hesitant. Then she kneeled down and touched the grass with the tip of her fingers. It felt warm. She moved her hand towards a patch that hadn't been affected. It was cool, slightly humid even. She frowned. It had been over two days since it happened, yet the dead grass felt like it had been set on fire just moments prior.

No one in the market had seen it happen. Everyone had been either manning a stall or in the crowd, watching the dance. A few had passed by that spot since and noticed the odd line of grass, but nobody could explain it. Of course, she figured, none of them had access to the same source of information she did, being a Sylvan Tongue. They mocked her for it, said she was insane to claim she could speak to plants, but she'd never been anything but proud of it herself. It was a gift, her parents always told her, from the gods themselves. And one does not reject such a thing. Now, if only everyone else felt the same way. She looked up at where the decorations had been, all hastily removed once the festival was called off, and sighed.

That night, she couldn't sleep. She tossed and turned, tried opening the window, closing the window, more blankets, less blankets. Nothing worked. After a while she gave up and went to sit on the window sill, looking outside. The late hour and the lack of movement outside masked the uncertainty and dread of recent events. It seemed, to her, a perfectly normal, peaceful night. She leaned back on the window and closed her eyes.

"My child."

The voice came from nowhere and she snapped her eyes open. It came from a tree, she was certain, as she didn't hear it in quite the same way she heard everything else. It wasn't the voice of any of the trees near her house. She looked at her friend nonetheless. It slept quietly. It was funny, she thought, how trees slept just like people. Of course, one couldn't tell from looking at them, as they have no faces, but she could sense it, even without touching it. Their connection was a strong one, after all.

"My child, do you hear me? Please, I have great need of your help."

The voice spoke again and she threw her legs over the window sill, held on to the sides and leaned out to look outside. When she still couldn't find the source of the voice, she tried to speak back. "Who are you?"

Silence.

She frowned and began to turn back when the voice came again.

"It is I, Life of All, Yrathea. My child, you who speaks to our kind, your assistance is of utmost importance right now."

Teiwa froze. Certainly that was a joke. Why would Yrathea need her, of all people? Even though Sylvan Tongues were rare, certainly there were others better equipped to help the Life of All with whatever she may need. Yet it was most certainly the voice of a tree. She felt it inside her, more than heard it. And trees never joked about such matters. It was the greatest disrespect to use the Sacred Tree's name in vain like that. She bit the inside of her lip.

"What assistance? What do you need from me?"

Again, her answer was silence for a time. Then the voice came, and she thought this time it sounded almost like it was crying.

"My child, I am dying."

2

REUNION

Days passed since Teiwa received the calling from Yrathea. She hadn't told anyone other than her parents. They were concerned, but believed her when she claimed there was no way the message could be fake, and were ultimately proud of their daughter.

"I've always known you were destined to do great things," her mother had said and her father had been quick to agree.

Still her heart was restless. She was only one person. Just a young woman, freshly out of her teenage years, who had never left her island. How was she to help, simply because of her magical affinity? Yrathea had assured her it was enough. That she was enough. It felt rude to argue with the Sacred Tree, blasphemous even, but she could not bring herself to agree. Worse yet, no one but the light elves knew the location of the Sacred City and the Holy Tree that resided within it, or so the stories told. She'd been assured she would feel drawn to it, that her power would guide her there, but she did not know what distance she would have to go, or what dangers she might encounter. To go on her own seemed simply impossible. And yet, she could not bear the thought of asking her father for any of the island guards to accompany her.

The world had been at peace for well over a thousand years, and armies were not needed, but all cities had their own guard to deal with any criminals that might appear. Eastlake was known for being safe and having an extremely low criminality rate, but what if that was due to their strong guard? What if taking guards away from the island meant its doom?

Perhaps she was being overly dramatic. Doom might be an exaggeration. But it could spell trouble, and she could never forgive herself if her actions caused any negative effects on the people she would someday come to lead. Not that she wanted to lead, but that was an entirely different issue, and her mind was already too full to worry about it now.

She walked with her head down as she thought of all things that could go wrong if she were to ask for help, when she bumped into someone's back. The person's long, voluminous curly hair stuck to her and she made a face as she spat them off. The woman in front of her turned around, one eyebrow raised.

"Excuse me?"

Teiwa looked up to her and was met with someone familiar. It was Urdara, one of her dear childhood friends. She'd moved away and they had not seen each other in years, but Teiwa had no doubt about it. With her dark skin, black hair and golden eyes—a sign of her affinity with fire magic—she was even more stunning than she'd been the last time Teiwa saw her. She wore dark, tight pants and a loose blouse, and even with her ears, the same shape as that of everyone on the island, she was a stark contrast to those around her, with their colorful dresses and skirts. Teiwa wondered, with a hint of amusement, which of the two looked more out of place.

Recognition flashed in Urdara's eyes.

"Teiwa?"

"It is you!" Teiwa jumped into her old friend and embraced her. Urdara made a sound of displeasure and pushed her away.

"Right, let's not do that."

Heat rose to Teiwa's cheeks and she shot her an apologetic smile. Just because she'd missed her friend—friends, even—dearly, did not mean they felt the same way. Certainly, with Urdara's natural charisma, she had not suffered the same friendless fate as her since she moved away. Teiwa had a million questions she wanted to ask, but decided to start with something that would hopefully not be too much of an intrusion.

"What are you doing here? Did you come for the festival? I'm afraid it ended early this year…" She grimaced at the memory of the festival's events that day.

"No, I'm here for information," Urdara replied. She paused for a moment, then snapped her fingers. "Actually, you might be able to help me with that."

Teiwa blinked. What information could she possibly be after that she couldn't find in a bigger city on the continent? Unless she was there to find out about the man who died. She had to know, but to ask flatly like that might not be the wisest.

"I'm happy to help," she said, "but first, where are you staying? At the inn? You know my parents would never forgive me if I didn't bring you to stay at our house. Why don't you come to dinner tonight, bring your things, and I'll be glad to assist you then." She grinned.

Urdara looked inconvenienced.

"Unless you would rather not." Teiwa regretted the offer. Perhaps it had been going too far. She wanted information, but she also desperately wanted to catch up with her friend, and she'd let that get in the way of her thinking. "But you know my parents would love to have you."

Her friend—former friend, she thought—watched her for a moment and sighed. "I don't know, I really only need this one piece of information and then I'm out of here. I mean no offense to you or your parents. You know I hold you all in the highest regard."

"What information do you need, then?" Teiwa asked, defeated.

Urdara scratched at her neck, clearly uncomfortable with the subject.

"I need to know where my family came from before moving here. I have reason to believe they lied to me about that, and I need to know the truth."

"The truth?"

Silence hung over the two for an uncomfortably long moment as Urdara apparently pondered whether to answer that question or not.

"I'm supposedly adopted," Urdara replied at last, a hint of venom in her voice, "but really, who's to say those people didn't just steal me from my real family?"

Teiwa's eyebrows shot up. Urdara's relationship with her family had always been a difficult one. It came as little surprise that she might not, after all, share their blood. But to accuse them of stealing her was an entirely different level.

"So you want access to my father's records," Teiwa said after a moment. "I can get you that. If you accept my offer to stay at our home and join us for dinner tonight." She smiled. Maybe she didn't have to give up on catching up after all.

Urdara crossed her arms, an amused expression on her face. "Really, that's how it's gonna be? All right, I'll take it. It is free stay and a meal, after all. Your loss, quite literally."

"So I have your word?"

"Yes, you have my word." She rolled her eyes.

"Awesome, let's go get your things then. I'm sure Ronas will understand."

One quick stop at the inn, a few minutes ensuring the innkeeper and his daughter that yes, she was fine—to Urdara's visible confusion—and one failed request for news of his son—her other childhood friend—later, they were on their way. As they stopped in front of the house, Teiwa placed her hand on the knob and turned back to face Urdara.

"Oh, and those records are public, by the way." She grinned.

Urdara laughed. "All right, you have my respect. Guess you still have it in you."

Teiwa's parents greeted Urdara with enthusiasm. They too hadn't seen her in years, and were as excited as their daughter to have her over like in the old days. Ashtari, especially, was quick to wrap her in a hug, which she responded to uncomfortably at first, but warmed up to. Teiwa's father, Neirrod, had a servant prepare more food so he could offer his guest a worthy dinner despite her protests that it was not necessary.

Unlike Ashtari, Neirrod was a large man. She wasn't short, but wasn't particularly tall either, and had a slim figure. He, on the other hand, was tall and imposing, with a wide build that was envied by many of the island guards. He kept his red hair long enough to reach his shoulder blades and tied back in numerous small braids, and his almost as long beard was carefully trimmed and styled in much the same manner. His green eyes sparkled in the same color as his daughter's, a sign of his sylvan magic, which he was very proud of. While he seemed intimidating to many, when Urdara looked at him she saw what she imagined Teiwa must see, a kind, loving father figure, with a laugh that could fill the entire room and the most generous heart of all.

She had never had a good relationship with her family, and as a child it had not been rare for her to spend time at her best friend's home instead. Teiwa's parents had accepted her immediately, having known her since she was a toddler. It occurred to her, as she thought about it, that they too might have information on her origins, regardless of the records Neirrod kept at his office in the town hall. She would have to ask them, when the opportunity presented itself.

Dinner was filled with joyful conversation and laughter as the group reminisced on memories of the two young women as children. Teiwa was mostly embarrassed by the stories, as they often focused on her getting into trouble as she dragged her friends into her little adventures. Urdara, meanwhile, relished her friend's discomfort and only laughed harder. When she could, she asked seemingly innocent questions to fish information from them without having to delve into the subject of her origins. Noticing she did not wish to discuss it in detail, Teiwa did not push to bring the subject to light, which she greatly appreciated. Perhaps agreeing to dinner—even if she had essentially been blackmailed into it—had not been so bad after all.

After the couple and the servants went to sleep, Teiwa and Urdara stayed behind, sitting on the couch drinking tea that had been left for them before everyone retired for the night. Ashtari had brought them blankets to wrap themselves in should they feel cold, even though it was summer. *Just a mom thing*, she'd said with a laugh.

"So what you're telling me is you're still the weird kid who talks to the trees, just older," Urdara remarked with a smirk.

"Really, that is what you got from that story?"

"I got many things from it," she said and took a sip of her tea, "but that's the only one that I knew would get on your nerves."

Teiwa groaned and rested her forehead against her cup.

"Anyway," Urdara continued, "how do you even know that was the Tree? You know, with the capital T."

"I can't tell if that's being disrespectful or not." Teiwa narrowed her eyes. "But I don't know, I mean… It felt different. It wasn't quite like when I talk to the trees around here, and I could tell it was coming from very far away. It takes a lot of magic to be able to communicate with someone that far from where you are. Besides, trees don't have a reason to prank me about that. They generally don't have a sense of humor. At all." She frowned, a variety of times she'd tried joking with them and failed flashing through her memories at once. They were good friends and very good listeners, but not particularly fun.

"So what are you going to do about it?" Urdara asked, her cheek resting against her fist as she leaned on the armrest.

"That's the thing, I have no idea. I can't just ask my father for some of the island guards, what if something happens? Especially now that there's a risk of other waves of forbidden magic hitting us. But I also can't do it on my own. I've never even left the island, how am I supposed to do anything?" Teiwa frowned. Her mother always told her not to be so hard on herself, but it was difficult not to when apparently the world's fate rested on her rather incompetent shoulders.

"You can always just hire a guide." She took a sip of her tea, still resting against her fist. "Back in the continent, there's the Traveler's Guild, or whatever. They have guides for hire that will take you wherever you want to go safely."

It was a good idea, there was just one tiny issue.

"But I don't know where exactly I'm supposed to go!" Teiwa cried.

Urdara stopped and stared at her.

"All right, now you're just being difficult."

Teiwa groaned. "It's not my fault... She just told me I would feel drawn towards her, that I would know the way. How do I hire someone to take me somewhere safely if I have to figure out where it is as I go?"

"I don't know, hire an escort then. There's probably a lot of people out there willing to take the job. Just get to the continent and I'm sure you'll find someone."

While Teiwa hoped she was right, part of her still felt hopeless. Even if she accepted the calling, what was she to do once she got there? She was just one person, and not even a particularly talented or strong one. There was nothing she could do. Surely, she thought, Yrathea had made a mistake.

The next morning, the two slept in. Neirrod would go to work early, and with Urdara not wanting to go into detail over her reason to be on the island, Teiwa figured it was best they wait until he was busy before they went to the city hall. Ashtari's shift at the hospital only started later in the day, but she'd joined her husband for breakfast and left early to run errands.

The city hall was an imposing building, or as imposing as it was possible within the island, where everything was bright and colorful. It was the biggest building they had, with a large dining hall capable of holding dozens of families, which was also used for public meetings, and a smaller area for public records to a side. The tower housed a messenger dragon and her baby, but they weren't often seen from the ground. During the day, her father stayed mostly on the second floor, in a smaller meeting room where he handled all sorts of matters with the villagers and his advisors.

As the two neared the building, Teiwa overheard a conversation between one of the nurses at the hospital and someone she didn't know. The woman sounded distressed.

"You go on ahead," she told Urdara, "I'll catch up to you, I just need to do something first."

Urdara shrugged and did as she was told. Teiwa approached the nurse and laid a hand on her shoulder.

"I'm sorry, I couldn't help but overhear. You were there when my mother treated that man from the festival? Or... Tried to, I suppose. I was wondering if you could tell me more about what happened to him."

The woman eyed her cautiously. "I'm sorry, my lady, I'm not sure Lady Ashtari would like me to disclose such upsetting information with you."

Teiwa took a deep breath and willed her voice to remain calm. "I understand, but I need to know so I can move on from the whole thing. Surely you can see my side. Please, I assure you my mother will not hear of this."

"My lady, that's— I don't think—" She sighed.

The man nodded to the woman and she looked all around them to ensure not only Ashtari wasn't around, but also anyone who may tell her about it. Teiwa joined in her search, just in case. When they felt it was safe, she spoke.

"We don't understand what happened to him. He was in so much pain when we brought him in, and we took off his shirt so we could search for injuries. But his stomach, it was..." She shuddered. "It was moving. You could actually see it move. Lady Ashtari used her magic to feel inside him, to try to grasp exactly what was happening, but she just screamed. He died shortly after. The other medic present worried he might have some sort of parasite and said we ought to open him, so if there was a threat to others, we would know before it reached that point, but your mother just kept begging him not to. We didn't understand why, until we cut him open."

Teiwa nodded, a sign for her to continue. She gulped.

"His... His insides." She paused to take a deep breath and Teiwa noticed she was holding back tears. "They were open, like flowers in bloom. Bloody, horrible flowers in bloom. I don't know what could have possibly caused it. We had his body burned. Not in the traditional ceremony as usual, just... Burned. We were too afraid he would spread whatever it was that he had. I hope Death can forgive us."

The information hit Teiwa like a punch and she stumbled back a step. She'd assumed he fell from somewhere at first, but even with the information that it had been forbidden magic, nothing could have prepared her for this. Her mind raced and amidst it all, one thought came to the surface.

"What about his family?" she asked.

The woman shook her head. "We couldn't identify him. No one seems to recognize him, so he was probably a visitor here for the festival. We don't know who to notify. We can only hope someone comes looking for him. Or perhaps..." She paused. "Perhaps it's best no one does. I cannot imagine losing one's family to something that horrible."

Teiwa nodded in agreement. She took the woman's hands in hers. "Thank you. I know it mustn't have been easy for you to tell me this."

The nurse shook her head and left without saying another word. The man beside her bowed in sign of respect and took off after her.

Teiwa stood there, frozen in place for a time. Then the fact she'd sent Urdara ahead came to mind and she rushed to meet her at the city hall.

"Ah! Lady Teiwa, here to see your father, I presume?" an older woman called out to her as she entered the building.

She tried to smile. It was far harder than she'd anticipated. "No, actually I'm here to see a friend. She's probably looking through the public records right now."

The woman smiled and nodded in understanding. She pointed her in the right direction and carried on with whatever she was doing. Teiwa appreciated that she didn't try to make small talk, though perhaps the look on her face was the reason for it. She couldn't possibly be looking well. It made sense to her now, why her mother hadn't gone into detail about it. She couldn't blame her for it, now that she knew what transpired. Perhaps she should have listened to her.

She found Urdara sitting at a desk, face resting against her fist and a purple flame lighting the desk as she went through the pages of a book with an absent look on her face. Teiwa took a seat beside her and grabbed the book at the top of the pile next to her.

"Find anything yet?"

"What do you think?" Urdara stopped to stare at her.

"All right, sorry I asked."

"Your father really keeps track of everything, huh. I asked for the records only for the years around when we supposedly moved here, and it's still a lot."

"Yes, I suppose he's meticulous with the history of our island." Teiwa tried to laugh. It came out a sad attempt. Urdara looked at her with a raised eyebrow.

"What's gotten into you?"

Teiwa shook her head and opened the book she'd taken. Urdara watched her for a moment, then shrugged and continued her reading.

Though she tried to help her friend, her mind was only partly in her reading. When Urdara called out to her to tell her she'd found what she was after, she only barely heard her in the background. Images of what the man's insides must have looked like flashed into her brain, along with the memories of his face, contorted in pain as he begged her for help. There had been nothing she could do for him. But there was something she could do to help others.

She had to accept Yrathea's calling.

3

COINCIDENCE

Though it was early in the morning when they reached the port, so many people walked past that Teiwa could have sworn it was the middle of the day. Despite the small number of ships that sailed from the island to the continent, it was busy and voices filled her ears from all sides.

"I found it!" one of the twins called out from before a ship.

"Of course you found it, there's barely any ships!" her twin brother yelled back at her.

"How do they have so much energy?" Kadi groaned and Teiwa suppressed a laugh. As the middle sister, it was often the blonde girl's job to watch the twins, and it was one she did not appreciate. Though they were a handful, Teiwa often wished she had siblings of her own. Her mother had struggled to carry a pregnancy to term, and though she was only blessed with one child, they had an altar at home for their lost family members which included the three older siblings Teiwa would have had, had the gods allowed. It was a custom her mother had brought from her homeland that others on the island often found morbid, but to Teiwa, it was a sign of love and respect. Still, it would feel better, she thought, to have siblings who could talk back when she spoke to them.

"You were the same when you were her age," Balri—the oldest—laughed, rubbing his sister's head and messing up her hair. She shot him a dirty look. "Absolutely terrible."

Urdara stood beside Teiwa, watching silently as her friend and her four cousins yelled and laughed back and forth at each other. She had three older brothers —triplets—but they'd never been her friends, and she had no cousins. That she knew of, she figured. After all, the family she'd grown up with was not her real family, and the men she called brothers had never been related to her any more than they acted it. She'd found the records at the city hall, proof that those she'd referred to as her parents her entire life had lied when she asked them about where they'd moved in from.

In truth, she already knew something was wrong. Not only because of how strained their relationship had always been, but because of a letter they'd received one day, from a town she hadn't heard of. It spoke of a house they'd abandoned and how it had been empty for so long that the town was reclaiming it. That much wasn't the problem, she knew they'd lived in various places before coming to Eastlake, but that they'd simply abandon a house rather than selling or even surrendering it back to the town was odd, and the end of the letter sent regards to "the boys". Not the children, but the boys. From the information on the letter, it had been clear that by the time they left the house, she'd already been a year old, so why would she not be included? That much got her mother to admit, upon being confronted about it, that she had been adopted, but she claimed they'd come from a different town entirely, that the house had belonged to a late family member and that they'd only lived there briefly a few years before her adoption. The records, however, were clear. They'd come from the town mentioned in the letter, right after she'd supposedly been brought into the family legally. If that was the case, however, why lie about it?

It was the lie that rattled. She hadn't cared to learn they weren't of the same blood, they'd never felt that way to her. But that they'd made a point to raise her as their own without ever giving her the truth about her origin was infuriating, to say the least. It was why, when Teiwa proposed they travel together, to her hometown and to Yrathea, in *whichever order works out* as she'd put it, that Urdara accepted. She could very well simply hire someone to take her, but somehow, despite the distance that had grown between them in the years since she moved away, traveling with an old friend simply felt safe.

"Are you nervous, dear?"

The voice came from her other side and pulled Urdara from her thoughts. She looked over to find Teiwa's aunt, Numa, smiling sweetly at her.

"Not really." She shrugged. "I just got distracted, that's all."

Numa made a soft sound of understanding and nodded. "It's going to be fine. You two will be together and I'm sure you'll help each other through whatever comes your way."

Now it was Urdara's turn to nod. Had the woman not believed her when she said she wasn't nervous, or did she notice something she hadn't herself? Perhaps it didn't matter.

Teiwa stopped in front of their ship and kneeled down, arms open wide. The twins jumped into a hug and she nearly fell backwards, laughing. Balri helped her stand and pulled her into a hug, himself.

"You be safe," he said, "and if anything happens, and I mean anything, I'll come running. Just send a message and I'll be there."

A smile tugged at the corner of her lips. "You know travel isn't that fast, right?"

"I said I'll be there."

She laughed. Kadi joined in the hug and soon her parents were rushing to hug their niece as well. Urdara stood back and said goodbye to Teiwa's parents, instead, before they too went to embrace their daughter themselves.

⁂

Travel to the continent wouldn't take long. The captain informed them they'd get there by sundown the next day, so long as the weather allowed it. Teiwa watched for a while as he talked to the mermaids that followed the ship and wished she understood it better. *Mermaids cannot speak the same way we do*, her other dear friend had taught her when they were children, *so the captain taught them sign language so we can still talk to them*. He'd made a point, then, to learn. She hadn't. It had never proven particularly necessary to her, but she regretted the choice nonetheless. Urdara had watched the scene too, only for a moment, before huffing and leaving for the berth she'd been assigned. When she didn't come back, Teiwa decided to go after her.

"There you are," she said.

Urdara rolled her eyes. "There's not many places I could be."

Teiwa shrugged and sat down beside her in her berth. "Are you all right?"

"Sure," she replied, "just wanted to try out the ship's beds. Speaking of beds..." She leaned towards Teiwa with a smile. "How do you want to handle beds during this journey? We could always share."

Teiwa cocked her head to the side. "Like when we were kids?"

"Definitely not like when we were kids."

The two sat in awkward silence for much longer than Urdara anticipated, or wanted.

"Oh!" Teiwa said. "Are you making a joke? I think I get it now."

Urdara shook her head and sighed in exasperation. "Only if you're not interested."

Teiwa blinked a couple times. Realization dawned upon her and heat crept to her face, ears and chest. "... Oh. Well... That's... I'm not really... I'm sorry?"

Urdara burst into laughter. "That's fine, just seeing that reaction was worth the rejection."

"I didn't realize you were interested in women," Teiwa said, trying to change the subject, and failing.

Urdara shrugged, uncaring. "I'm interested in people. I don't really care what they are, so long as they're attractive. Guess that's not how you work, though. But you know where to find me if you change your mind." She winked at her. "Now get off my bed so I can take a nap."

Teiwa blinked again and did as she was told.

⚘⚘⚘⚘⚘ — ⚘⚘⚘⚘⚘

As the captain predicted, travel was short and uneventful. The weather remained good for the duration of the journey and they reached the port at Baysea by sunset the day after departure. The passengers disembarked without issue and since they didn't have any cargo to unload, Teiwa and Urdara were able to leave the ship quickly.

The city was lively, with its white buildings and stony pathways, and soon Teiwa and Urdara were sitting on a fountain in the middle of a square. They watched people mill about for a time as they discussed their options. It was getting dark, and though it didn't seem the city was anywhere close to going to sleep, it was probably best that they arranged a place for them to do so that night. They could find a guide and buy all the supplies they'd need in the morning, when they weren't at risk of being left to sleep on the street for getting lost.

Though the square near the port had been difficult to navigate with how busy it was, once they moved farther away movement came more easily. There were still people on the streets, but nowhere near as many and they could more easily find someone willing to give them directions. The fact that Urdara had been to the city a number of times also helped. She did not know exactly where the things they needed were, but she had a good notion to move around without getting lost and to their joy, the streets had indicators on every corner, naming their location and on most of them, giving directions to the most important buildings in the city.

The first inn they tried was already at full capacity, confirming their fears that they might not have a place to sleep, should they dally. The second inn, not too far from the first, was bustling with life when they walked in. The many tables in the main hall were full of people eating, drinking and laughing. A young woman moved swiftly between tables, taking orders, and directed them to the counter to discuss accommodations with the owner when asked. She seemed sweet enough, but as they passed by her, Teiwa caught her smacking one of the customers. She didn't see why, but she figured he ought to have deserved it.

They approached the counter, already expecting to hear there was no room for them. The owner was a large woman, wide and muscular, with a big smile and hair so yellow it reminded Teiwa of the gold fabrics woven by goldweaving spiders, a rare material she was lucky enough to have as accents in a few of her nicer dresses. On the counter rested a guinatee, a small critter with soft fur and a small, curved beak, known for their ability to send messages to others of their kind through magic. They were all connected, Teiwa's father had explained to her, and if well treated were happy to relay messages to all over the continent. If you mistreated one, however, they had a tendency to be loud screamers. The one on the counter sat still and looked content, and Teiwa thought it would be good to send a message home, after they arranged for a place to stay.

Despite their fears, the inn did have rooms available. They booked one single room for the two of them, but with separate beds, at Urdara's request. She laughed about it, and the innkeeper only nodded along, not understanding what might be so funny about that.

"We're serving dinner right now," the woman offered, "if you're hungry. You're free to drop your things off in your room and come find a table for yourselves."

Teiwa stretched a hand out towards Urdara. "Give me your bag, I'll go up and you find us a spot. I'll be right back."

Urdara handed her the bag and watched as she ran up the stairs, bags on her shoulders and the room key in her hand. A moment too late, it occurred to her to ask if it was possible to eat in the room. The innkeeper was now gone from the counter and she leaned against it to wait for her return. From the corner of her eye, movement caught her attention and she turned to see a young human man doing the same. He was tall and handsome, with his dark skin, black hair at chin length and eyes every bit as golden as hers. He looked back to a table behind him and laughed, signaling for them to wait. She stared. Feeling watched, he stopped to look at her as he turned back towards the counter. She narrowed her eyes and looked down at his neck, where a golden ring hung from a simple chain. He opened his mouth to speak, but she didn't give him a chance.

"It's you," she declared so angrily that he took a step back, eyes wide.

From the table, his friends caught sight of the situation and laughed. "What did you do this time, Stick?" called out one of the men.

"I didn't—I don't…" he replied, confused, then turned to look at Urdara again. A spark of recognition lit his eyes and she only looked angrier for it. "Dara?"

"Don't you 'Dara' me. What are you doing here? I thought you were dead! How dare you not be dead?" she yelled and the people around stopped their meals and conversation to watch.

A number of them stood from their tables.

"Is something the matter here?" a man asked.

Before either could answer, another voice came from the stairs.

"Alright, time for dinner," Teiwa announced to no one in a singsong tone, before stopping dead in her tracks at the sight of the dinner hall. "What's going on?" she asked slowly.

Urdara didn't know his eyes could get any wider, but they did. His head snapped to the side and he gaped at Teiwa.

"Hey, don't you look at her!" Urdara snarled. He didn't listen.

His mouth worked a moment, but no words came out. Teiwa stood on the staircase, one foot on each step, staring with eyes as wide as his.

"Tei," he breathed. "Tei, I—" Teiwa opened her mouth to speak at the same time as him, just as shocked to see her old friend. And right after meeting Urdara again, too. It had to be fate.

Urdara cut him off with a slap to the face.

"Urd!" Teiwa called out and rushed down the stairs. "What is wrong with you?"

He held a hand to his face and looked at the two, more hurt showing in his eyes than in the mark on his cheek. "I suppose I had that coming."

"Damn right, you did!" Urdara yelled and rushed out the back door. Teiwa hadn't even realized there was a back door and wondered for a moment if her friend had just stormed into the kitchen, or perhaps a closet.

The young man chased after her a moment later and Teiwa blinked and ran after him.

Everyone in the dinner hall was left in a confused silence.

Despite having gone after them only a moment later, Teiwa was far behind enough that she could barely make out their shapes in the dark. The back door led to a wooded area and Urdara had run towards the trees. Of course. She followed their silhouettes for a time before they suddenly disappeared. Confused, she kept running, only to be met with a crater on the ground. Too late to stop, she fell in face first, rolled down over something—or someone, judging by the complaint she heard on her way down—and landed on the ground beside her friend.

"And there goes our chance of getting out," a disgruntled Urdara announced, lying on her back on the floor of the crater, covered in dirt.

"It's not my fault you decided running into the woods was somehow a good reaction to an upsetting encounter with an old friend," the young man claimed, practically upside down as he lay on the bottom of the wall of the crater, trying to wiggle his way into a more acceptable position.

"You are not my friend, At'lokias," she said his name with a tone of disgust and he groaned.

"Fine! An ex old friend. Are you happy now?" he asked, exasperated.

"No, because I'm trapped in here with you!"

Teiwa sighed deeply and rested her face on the dirt. It was still better than listening to the bickering. When it felt like long enough since the two had stopped, she pushed herself up and sat down. By then, At'lokias had managed to move from the wall to the floor of the crater and was sitting as well. Urdara remained as she was.

"Alright, now you're just being dramatic." Teiwa rolled her eyes. "Stop it."

"I will stop when I want to." She crossed her arms.

Teiwa and At'lokias both groaned at the same time, then looked at each other and snorted.

"It's not funny!" Urdara called out in indignation.

"This is probably the most idiotic situation I have ever been in," At'lokias said between laughs, "and I have been in some really stupid ones."

The two laughed for a time, despite Urdara's protests. When it died down, Teiwa looked up at the night sky and sighed.

"What happened to us?" she asked.

"We fell down a hole," At'lokias replied and she slapped his arm.

"He left, that's what happened." Urdara turned to face away from them.

"You left too, you know," Teiwa said, her voice low. Urdara opened her mouth to protest, but Teiwa continued. "I was all alone." She pulled her knees up and hugged them, a quiet sniffle escaping her.

Silence filled the space between the three of them.

"I'm sorry," At'lokias said at last.

"Sorry doesn't fix anything," Urdara replied. "You left without saying anything. We went to see you one morning and you were just gone without a single word. Not even a note. Even your father didn't know where you had gone off to. Sure, I moved away, but that's different. My family moved away, I didn't get a choice, and I said goodbye. But you? You just left us. Like we were nothing. You left." Her voice cracked at the last word and she cleared her throat to try and hide the tears that were welling up in her eyes.

"I know," he said simply.

Teiwa hugged her knees tighter, tears brimming on her eyelashes.

"I know it was awful of me to do that," he continued. "And it kills me to know that I hurt you two, but I know I did. I don't expect you to believe me, and I certainly don't expect you to forgive me. I did what I had to do. I had a reason, a very, very important reason, and I can't tell you what it is.

At least not yet. And I wish there had been another way, but there wasn't, so I don't regret it. I would have done it again. I'm sorry."

Urdara's head snapped in his direction and she sat up to hit him. She slapped at him to the best of her ability, which wasn't great, but he let her. Teiwa sat in silence for a time.

"I forgive you," she said, her voice barely above a whisper.

Urdara stopped her aggression and she and At'lokias both turned to face her. At'lokias' eyes widened. "You do?" he asked.

She nodded her head, then realized they may not be able to tell in the dark and said it out loud as well. "I do."

At'lokias' eyes filled with tears. "Thank you," he cried. "Thank you so much."

Urdara sat back on her heels. She stared down at the ground, her hands in fists over her thighs. "Well, I don't."

At'lokias took a moment to answer. "That's your right," he said at last. "Now, we should probably figure out a way to get out of here."

"You know, for all those people looked concerned about you back at the inn, nobody came after us," Urdara grumbled.

"Urd!" Teiwa exclaimed.

"What? It's true. From how they reacted, you'd think they cared." Urdara grinned.

"To be fair, I am always getting in trouble, and I have yet to die from it." At'lokias shrugged.

"Ah, yes. That is very reassuring. I trust you completely now." She rolled her eyes. Teiwa glared at her, but she either couldn't tell in the dark, or ignored it.

"What do you think made this hole anyway?" At'lokias said in an attempt to guide the subject back in a useful direction.

"It looks like a den," Teiwa said. "Some smaller dragons like to make dens like this under trees whose roots are above ground. The tree must have moved elsewhere, leaving the den unprotected."

Urdara made a face. "If it's going to move, the least it could do is cover the hole back so this kind of thing doesn't happen."

"Maybe it didn't expect a bunch of idiots to come running into the woods after dark," At'lokias retorted with a grin.

"Either way, there's other trees nearby. If I can just..." Teiwa felt around the earth with her hands for a moment, then dug into the wall until she had a hole she could stick her hand in. She found a root and held on to it.

"Are you going to do your weird thing?" Urdara asked.

"I am already 'doing my weird thing', so be quiet so I can hear."

Urdara crossed her arms and huffed, but said nothing more. A few moments passed in silence before a rumbling caught her attention. She looked up to see a tree leaning forward into the hole and held back a yelp.

The tree reached in as far as it could and left its branches hanging.

"There you go, my 'weird thing' has gotten us help," Teiwa said, took hold of a branch, and climbed out of the hole.

"Ladies first," At'lokias announced with a dramatic gesture towards the tree.

Urdara huffed and climbed out as well. She had half a mind to push him back into the hole once he followed, but figured it wouldn't go well with Teiwa and decided against it, to her chagrin. Once they were all out, Teiwa touched her forehead to the tree and mouthed a thank you. The tree returned to its original position and did not move again.

Everyone in the dinner hall stopped their conversations again as the three entered through the back door, disgruntled and covered in dirt. At least one person snickered. The innkeeper rushed over to them, horrified.

"By the Gods, what happened to you three?"

"She did," At'lokias pointed at Urdara with his thumb. She had to fight back the urge to throttle him.

"We fell into a hole in the woods," Teiwa added, much more helpful.

"You poor things, how about I draw you a bath? It will only take a moment." She did not give them time to answer before she rushed to the kitchen to ask for help with the hot water.

"Well, I guess I'm going then." At'lokias pointed to the front door.

"Going? Aren't you staying here at the inn?" Teiwa asked, her head tilted to one side.

"Oh, no. I just come here with my coworkers for food and drinks sometimes. I stay at the headquarters at my work."

Teiwa blinked. "And what do you do, exactly?"

The answer he gave filled Urdara with dread.

"I work for the Travelers' Guild. I'm a guide."

4

MEETING

At'lokias was eight years old when the life he knew came to an end.

It was an honest mistake, though one that should have been easily avoidable by any experienced sailor. The seafoam dragon had been swimming close to the ship—too close for comfort, the man had decided—and in his panic, he shot a harpoon at it. Had he been older, more knowledgeable, he would have known better than to attack a creature known for being docile, and for guiding ships such as theirs to safety during storms, such as the one they faced. But the captain had him on deck at the time, and he'd been close to the harpoon—only there for emergencies, really—and the fear was stronger than any logic.

The dragon did not take kindly to being shot at. Hurt, both its body and its heart, it lashed out against the ship in all its might. The vessel didn't stand a chance.

The first part to be hit was the side of the ship, with its glass windows just below water, a novelty they'd been proudly announcing just before the trip. A small At'lokias had been sitting in one of the berths with his baby sister as his twin brother looked out the window.

"Atty, you ought to come see this, it's amazing! I can see under the water!" the little boy exclaimed, excitement clear on his face as he turned to face his brother.

At'lokias shot a nervous grin back at him. "I can see from here. Besides, someone has to watch Sailo'e." He laughed as his older siblings glared at him. He was clearly using her as an excuse, and calling them useless in the process. He'd always been nervous around water and even getting him into the ship had been a challenge. It had been that way ever since he was younger, when he was out playing with his brother and ended up falling into a well.

"It's not the same," his twin brother protested. "Come, you have to see—"

An explosion of glass and water took the boy immediately. At'lokias' older siblings, horrified, jumped to their feet and dragged him up the stairs as fast as they could as the sailors below deck ran, some to patch the hole, others to escape.

Above deck was no better, as people ran in a frenzy in all directions. At'lokias caught sight of his mother as she rushed towards him and his siblings, but the dragon's tail hit the path between the two, separating the deck in two. Crossing was impossible. She screamed for them and they did for her as the hole in their path became wider by the minute. He thought he saw his father running in the background with the crew, but the scene was too chaotic to be certain. The only thing he did feel certain of was that they were doomed.

The ship went under moments after. The waters were vicious and freezing cold. At'lokias tried to swim to the surface while holding his baby sister, but he couldn't tell which way was up as he was tossed about under the waves. Even if he could, it would be nearly impossible to swim without using his arms. Debris from the ship hit him and he saw a shape swimming towards them as everything went black.

When he awoke, he was in an unfamiliar room. A hospital room, he soon learned from the sweet lady who had been waiting for him to come to, that he'd been brought to after a search party found him unconscious on the beach. Why there had been a search party at all was beyond him. He was in Eastlake, an elven island, and had been one of few people found still alive. When he asked where the others were, the lady went quiet and he knew. They hadn't made it. Not a single one.

He'd been found with a young woman holding on to him. The only other survivor. A mermaid. And from the way her tail and fins had dissolved, it was clear she'd clung to him all night, probably to help keep him warm. She'd saved his life. He couldn't tell if that was good or not.

He was alone. His entire family was gone, taken away from him in an instant. And who was he without them? He'd only ever been a son, a brother. Never on his own.

She asked if he'd like a moment alone and he nodded.

He was only eight years old. A child. It wasn't fair. It wasn't right. It was one thing for a child to bury their parents, when they'd grown old and their time had come. But to lose one's entire family in one fell swoop was unnatural. Where was he to go from here? He could ask to be taken back to his hometown, he supposed. Among his family's friends there was bound to be someone willing to take him in. But the idea of going back home without them felt wrong. He could ask to stay, see if anyone there would accept him instead, but that also felt wrong.

Being alive felt wrong. She closed the door and he screamed.

At'lokias didn't know how long he'd been sitting there, staring out the window and out of tears to cry when he heard the door open. He turned to look and saw the head of a child peeking in. He tilted his own to the side in curiosity, and apparently the child took it as an invitation to come inside. A boy, it seemed, with his short auburn hair and loose clothes, only about a year younger than him.

He sat on his bed and gave him a wide, warm smile. "Hi, I'm Teiwa! What's your name?"

The question caught him off guard and he blinked. He thought for a moment, processing the boy's words. It was an unusual name. The common form, as far as At'lokias knew, was Teiwal. A strong name, not at all fitting of the scrawny looking kid in front of him. Still, he figured, most children didn't look particularly strong, so it was not likely to be fitting for anyone at that age.

The boy looked at him expectantly and he remembered the question. "Right!" he exclaimed, "I'm At'lokias." He opened his mouth to continue, but changed his mind. He was going to tell the boy that he could call him Atty, but that was what his family called him. He never wanted anyone to use it ever again.

"Oh, that's such a cool name!" The boy beamed up. "Can I call you Loki? Everyone calls me Tei, so you can call me that too." He gasped, for no apparent reason, and his emerald eyes lit up. "Your eyes are so pretty! You're a fire elemental, right? My best friend is a fire elemental too. Her name is Urdara. I think you'll like her! She looks like you, but she's a girl. I'm a sylvan elemental, but you can probably tell."

He felt dizzy with all the information. Still, there was something soothing about the odd child. That he'd chosen to comment on his eyes, but not on his ears, came as a relief. He'd learned about Eastlake before. It was an all elven island, so it would make sense that he would be treated strangely for being human. And yet, this child didn't seem to care about it in the slightest. He'd been far more concerned with the color of his eyes, and not in a prejudiced way either. He didn't know how to answer, but the boy's joy seemed so contagious, he couldn't help a laugh.

The door opened and the lady from before walked in and gasped. "Teiwa! I told you to wait for me downstairs! What are you doing here, bothering my patient?"

"Oops," was all Teiwa said in response. He stood from the bed and ran to hide behind his mother.

"I'm so sorry," the lady continued, "you wanted time alone and here comes my daughter to drive you crazy. Please, forgive her."

Daughter. The word hit him like a slap to the face and he stared. He'd been so certain she was a boy. That explained the name, he supposed. It was a variation. Not one he knew, but perhaps common there. Still he couldn't stop looking at her, as she smiled apologetically at him from behind her mother.

"It's all right," he managed to say. "He, I mean, she didn't bother me." Then he thought for a moment and continued. "She can come visit again, if she wants."

Teiwa beamed up at him, and he felt a strange warmth in his chest. He smiled back.

A few days later, the young woman appeared at his room again with another visitor. This time it was a large man, also an elf, but with skin darker than At'lokias'. He had a bald head and wore an apron. He smiled gently and approached the boy with care.

"Hi there, little guy," he started. "My name is Ronas, and I'm the innkeeper here on the island. I've been told your name is At'lokias?"

At'lokias eyed him suspiciously, but nodded.

"Lady Ashtari here has told me about your situation. I'm very sorry."

The boy lowered his head and nodded again. When he said nothing, Ronas continued.

"I'm here because I want to make you an offer."

Once he was cleared from the hospital, At'lokias was taken to Ronas' inn. The man had offered to take him in as his own, and the boy had accepted to give it a try for a few days and see how it went. He wasn't sure why he didn't say no, but something on the island seemed to have a hold on him, for he considered less and less the possibility of going back to his hometown.

Ronas was a kind man. He had a daughter, Dido, who was a little older than At'lokias. At first, the boy hesitated to be taken in by a stranger, to be part of a new family. A couple of days into their experiment, Ronas told him of his wife who had died in labor.

"I know it's not the same," he'd said, "but we know the pain you're feeling."

And At'lokias felt he really understood. If there was a family out there for him, it ought to be a broken one like Ronas and Dido's.

It didn't take long for Teiwa to start visiting him at the inn and bringing her friend Urdara along. He hesitated around the new girl at first, but had already warmed up to Teiwa. One morning after breakfast, the two girls came to pick him up to play. Dido was cleaning tables and Ronas ran through a safety checklist with him before waving goodbye. As he walked out the door laughing, he thought maybe he could belong there after all.

At'lokias' mind was heavy with thoughts of his early life in Eastlake when he finished his bath and walked towards the rooms in the Traveler's Guild headquarters. From the death of his first family to being taken in by Ronas, and befriending Teiwa and Urdara. As he passed by, his boss and adoptive grandmother—a small but oddly imposing old elven lady—wished him good night from the main hall as she organized papers and he nodded in return. His friends were mostly asleep by the time he reached their quarters and he tossed himself on the bed and stared up at the ceiling.

He'd never expected to see them again. He certainly hoped he would someday, but not before he was done with his mission. At'lokias cursed in silence. He thought he'd have more time. He should have had more time. He stroked the short beard that lined his bottom jaw and sighed.

Urdara looked much like he'd assumed she would. Her anger too, had been predictable. He never expected her to take his sudden leave well. Though it stung to be told she expected him to be dead, he couldn't blame her for it, nor could he hold her refusal to forgive him against her. It had been something he brought upon himself and that he knew would happen when he made his choice. Still, the price would have been worth paying, had he had enough time to finish what he started. That he didn't was what truly bothered him.

Teiwa, on the other hand, was so different from how he'd expected that it was almost hilarious. He hadn't thought she would still look like a boy by now, she hadn't already when he left, but she'd grown to be much more feminine and womanly. She was more beautiful than he'd ever anticipated, and he hated it. The way her eyes sparkled when she smiled at him made his chest hurt.

And she'd forgiven him. After everything, after all those years. She'd forgiven him. She'd said she wanted to see him again the next day. He didn't know how good of an idea it was, but he couldn't possibly say no to her after all that. He'd never been good at denying her anything, whether he owed her or not.

He already half expected her to ask him to guide them. It was simply too much of a coincidence that they'd both be out in Baysea together if not for the purpose he expected, but still he hoped. If they were there for a different reason, any other reason, then there was still time. He would gladly take them wherever they had to go and go back to his mission. It was unlikely, but in the end he had no way of knowing yet. He tried to hold on to the hope of that uncertainty.

There was only one thing he was absolutely certain of, one thing that ate at him.

He still loved her.

❧ ❧

"This is probably the worst idea I can possibly think of, and I can think of several bad ideas you might have," Urdara said to Teiwa just as At'lokias walked over to the fountain they'd agreed to meet at. After the events of the previous night, Urdara had thought it would be best not to worsen her image by meeting at the inn again. While Teiwa had not approved of her reasons, she agreed to it.

"What is?" He flashed them a knowing smile.

"You are," Urdara snarled. He laughed.

"Don't you see?" Teiwa started. "It's not a bad idea! It's fate. Fate has brought us together for this."

"First of all, everyone knows Fate's actual name is Chaos, and she's evil, so I'm not sure how that's an argument in his favor." Urdara protested. "Then again, I guess that's exactly why you're right about this."

At'lokias made a face at that. *It better not be the case*, he thought.

If Teiwa noticed the change in his expression, she didn't show it, seeming more frustrated with Urdara instead. Urdara on the other hand looked at him with interest. He tried to return to a neutral expression. She looked even more interested.

"So what exactly is this you need a guide for, anyway?" he asked, hopeful.

Please let it be just some random trip, please let it be just some random trip, he chanted in his mind.

"Here, sit." Teiwa patted the fountain beside her and he hesitated for a moment before doing as he was told. "I'll explain everything."

She recounted everything, from her vision at the festival, to her agreement with Urdara to travel together, to their arrival at Baysea. He listened silently, careful not to let his frustration show.

"So this is why we need you," Teiwa continued, "and why it has to be you."

Urdara made a face. "What? Who says it has to be him?"

"Of course," Teiwa replied. "First of all, who other than a friend will take a job that requires no pre-defined plan like that? Plus, we know we can trust him."

"I don't know if that's a good idea—" he began.

Urdara interrupted him with a loud snort. "Trust him? Sure, maybe we can trust him not to kill us in our sleep, but who's to say he won't just leave us in the middle of nowhere?"

"All right, you know what? I understand that you can't forgive me, but this is ridiculous," At'lokias protested. "I'm not going to leave you in the middle of nowhere, I'm not going to leave you anywhere. I told you I had a very important reason to leave the island, that's not something I did for the fun of it. I'm a good person, and I take my job very seriously. If I get hired to take someone somewhere, you can be damn sure they get to their destination safely."

"So you do want to take us?" Urdara's eyes narrowed.

Fuck.

5

INJURY

At'lokias thought back on their earlier encounter with a sigh.

"So, what do you say?" Teiwa had asked him, hopeful, with a hand outstretched to him.

He'd hesitated. After a moment, he shook her hand. "Let's go."

Though he regretted having accepted the job, even if it was *somewhat* by accident, At'lokias couldn't deny that if anyone had to take them on their journey, he would rather be the one to do it than trust them to anyone else. His coworkers were good, trustworthy people, but this meant he could make sure they were safe at all times. Besides, if he hadn't fallen victim to his ego, he probably would have still accepted once Teiwa insisted on it, which she certainly would have.

While Urdara looked unhappy about it, she seemed to accept the decision, and he wondered how much of it was because she was intrigued. He'd been careless in his reactions and it had caught her attention, and he could only assume she wanted to investigate and find out what he was hiding. He'd have to be more careful from here on out.

Collecting supplies for the first leg of the journey was easier on his own, and so he had the two wait at the inn while he went shopping. He met with them at first light and they left as soon as they finished eating their breakfast. The road to the next city over—in the vague direction Teiwa pointed out—wasn't long, but it was heavily wooded and best traveled in daylight to avoid wild animals.

"Aren't we going to take any supplies with us?" Teiwa asked, eyeing At'lokias' strangely empty looking bag as they started the walk towards the city limits.

"You can, if you want to. But first I have something neat to show you two, just not here." He grinned.

"That doesn't sound suspicious at all," Urdara put in.

He rolled his eyes. "It's nothing like whatever you might be thinking, I assure you."

He guided them through the cobblestone streets with practiced ease, never stopping to check their whereabouts. The city came easily to him, after years of navigating it. They didn't comment on it and he was glad for that. It was best that they not know, at least not yet, that he'd been living in the very first city next to Eastlake for all these years. Perhaps later, when the hurt had subsided some, he might bring it up.

As they left the city and walked into the wooded road, At'lokias stopped and turned to them with a dramatic twist and a grin on his face. "All right, look at this."

He opened his bag, stuck his hand in, and pulled out another, identical bag from the inside. His bag's appearance didn't change in the slightest to indicate he'd removed anything from it. The two women raised eyebrows and watched with curiosity, but didn't react beyond that. At'lokias tossed the second bag to Teiwa with a wink and she caught it mid-air. He put his hand in the bag again and pulled yet another identical bag, and once again the appearance of his own bag remained the same. Now their eyes widened and they exchanged confused glances before looking back at him for answers.

"This," he began, "is a perk you only get by hiring me. None of the other guides have these."

"What in the world are those?" Urdara asked. He tossed the third bag to her and she caught it and shook it, trying to find what the trick might be.

"They're magical," At'lokias replied. "I got them from a light elf I'm friends with. They use these all the time. They're lined with silk from a special spider that lives in the Sacred City and infused with magic from the light elves themselves. You can fit as many things as you want inside. Isn't it amazing?"

"It's something, all right." Urdara turned it upside down in her inspection. "How do you find anything in there after?"

"You can always find what you want just by thinking about it as you reach in." He shrugged. "It's extremely practical. Now, I can't let you keep these, but you can use them for the duration of our journey. Like I said, a perk of having me as your guide." He winked at Teiwa again and she grinned back at him.

"This is incredible, Loki," she exclaimed. "Thank you. It will really come in handy."

"Speaking of journey," Urdara began as she opened the bag to peer inside. "How in the world does this... It looks empty. Why?" She shook it upside down, but nothing fell out.

"Oh, yours is empty. I have all the supplies with me." He laughed, earning himself a glare from her. "You're welcome to take some of them if you want, but it really doesn't weigh much more than an empty bag. I suggest just using yours to carry your own things. Your clothes and what have you."

"Anyway," she continued. "Speaking of, we haven't discussed the price for your... Services." She narrowed her eyes at him. "Surely you don't mean to charge us a fortune after the journey is over? We'll have to discuss costs beforehand. You understand."

"I do understand, Urdara," he said, her name heavy on his tongue. "I assure you I already thought long and hard about it. It's difficult to calculate costs on a journey that has no defined end in sight. So I was thinking we could agree on a price per day."

Urdara crossed her arms, her face stony. Teiwa watched the two, much more nervous than she felt she ought to be.

"Very well," she replied. "And how much do you intend to charge us per day?"

He lifted a finger in the air and grinned. "One smile from each."

Urdara groaned loudly and he broke into laughter. "That is the corniest thing I've ever heard! You can't be serious," she complained.

"I am. You can try to negotiate, if you'd like, but I'm not going below one smile from Tei a day. Oh hey, that rhymes."

Urdara covered her face with her palms and made a frustrated noise. Teiwa held back a laugh.

"Really, now, Loki. How much a day?" Teiwa asked.

"I'm dead serious. I'm not taking your money. You can save it for food and your stay at inns when we stop at cities. I'll pay for my own costs." She opened her mouth to protest, but he raised a hand to quiet her. "And that is not open for negotiation."

⁂

The three of them continued their travel down the wooded road for a time. Despite Urdara's protests, they did not stop to rest during the day, though At'lokias offered them food and water to consume while they walked. The road was reasonably well kept, with very few plants and rocks on the actual trail and a well defined path of hard packed soil. The trees loomed tall over them and filtered the sunlight so it was never too strong, but it was still easy to see where they were headed. Now and then he stopped them to check trails on their way and ensure there were no animals nearby that could cause any harm.

In order to make the best time, At'lokias suggested they continue walking past sundown for a while. They would camp at a clearing not too far ahead and continue walking first thing in the morning. Urdara made a face at the notion of camping, but there was nothing to be done about it. Whether she liked it or not, it was bound to be part of their journey sooner or later.

Not long after his suggestion, they came upon a tree standing in the middle of the road.

"Well," he said, "that's odd."

"Let me see what the problem is," Teiwa replied and walked over to the tree before he could say anything.

The tree moved tentatively from one side to another as she approached. At'lokias crossed his arms and watched.

"It's trying to block the path," he said.

"Wasn't that obvious from it being in the middle of the road?" Urdara rolled her eyes.

"Who knows, it could have been waiting around to ask for directions." He grinned and she groaned in return.

Teiwa spoke in a murmur and they failed to hear what she said. The tree spoke in its own language, which they couldn't even hear, so they didn't catch that part of the conversation either. She came back to them and took a moment to realize that fact.

"Oh, right. Sorry," she said. "It won't let us through for now. It says it can feel a wave of forbidden magic coming this way and it's not safe, so we have to wait."

Urdara frowned. "Who does that tree think it is to decide whether we can pass or not?"

"I'm quite certain it thinks it is a tree," At'lokias replied.

"Well, I'm not having any of it. Come on," Urdara said and moved towards the tree. It swayed to the sides as it tried to determine which way she would try to pass through.

"Urdara, just wait it out. It'll let us through as soon as it feels it's safe," Teiwa said, concern clear in her voice. "It's really not worth the risk."

"It said the wave is coming this way, right? So it's not here yet. We just need to pass first." Urdara crossed her arms in front of her chest and narrowed her eyes as she stared at the tree. "I don't know you, but I don't plan on walking around in the dark any longer than I have to. If we have to camp, let's get to that clearing already so we can do that."

At'lokias sighed and ran a hand through his hair. If he said anything against her plan, it would probably only further convince her to go through with it. But if he tried reverse psychology, she would just use it against him to say he agrees with her. Being quiet didn't feel like a great option either, but it was probably the safest one.

"Urd, come on, let's just wait. It'll probably be over soon." Teiwa sounded more distraught this time.

"No," was all Urdara said. She feinted running to one side and the three rushed in that direction. Once it was on the move, Urdara changed directions and jumped over its roots and into the road.

The moment her foot touched the ground, pain hit her like lightning and she screamed. Her left foot felt glued to the ground and wouldn't lift, no matter how she pulled, and the pain spread throughout her body. Teiwa called out to her, screaming, and tried to run towards her. At'lokias held out an arm to stop her.

"Wait, I got this."

He spat a curse and ran, using the tree's roots as an impulse as he jumped towards Urdara. The force of the impact threw them both on the ground and they rolled a fair distance from where she'd originally landed. Teiwa ran over to the tree and watched in fearful, uneasy silence.

At'lokias raised a thumb up to confirm they'd survived and she let out a breath of relief.

"I'm fine!" he called out.

The tree, frustrated at their shenanigans, refused to let Teiwa attempt to catch up to them, and so she leaned against it and waited as he held out a couple of fingers to Urdara's neck.

"She's alive," he yelled towards Teiwa, "but she's unconscious. We have to get her help."

"What do I do? I can't move from here."

At'lokias looked around and huffed. "I don't know how long it's going to be. It can't wait. The clearing is just ahead down this road, do you think you can make it there on your own?"

Teiwa shook her head vigorously. "No, please don't leave me."

"I'll come back for you! I swear," he said, his voice softer.

Teiwa's hands curled into fists and she shook her head again. "No."

"Then what would you have me do? We're wasting time arguing."

"Move her out of the way."

"Out of the way of what?" His eyes narrowed. When she didn't answer, he obeyed, just in case.

Teiwa ran back a few steps and turned to face him again. His eyes widened.

"Oh, no. You're not going to jump that. With our luck, you'll trip on the root and fall flat on your face."

"I've never tripped on a root in my life." She rolled her shoulders, took a deep breath, and ran. The tree lowered its roots in preparation. At'lokias watched in shock as her foot touched the root and the tree launched her up and forward with strength beyond what he anticipated. "Catch me!" she called out in the air and he scrambled to open his arms in time. She hit him and they both fell backwards onto the ground.

At'lokias lay on his back, groaning. Everything hurt, and he still had all her weight on top of him. She leaned up and looked back to where she'd come from with a wide smile on her face. "I did it!"

"Yes, you did. Now would you mind getting off me?" he asked with another groan.

She made a surprised sound as if she'd forgotten he was there, but was quick to do as he asked. Once she was on her feet, she offered him a hand with an apologetic smile.

As At'lokias picked Urdara up and rushed down the road with Teiwa on his heels, the tree moved out of the road. The wave had passed while they argued, but she'd seemed so determined, it didn't feel right ruining the moment. They'd never find out, anyway.

❧⸗⸗⸗ ⸗⸗⸗☙

"I'm sorry, I can't find anything wrong with your friend. I don't know why she's unconscious. There are no injuries, no scars; she doesn't seem to be in pain either. My guess is she passed out from exhaustion. She can stay here overnight and we'll keep an eye on her, but I imagine she'll be out and about again by morning." The medic at the hospital in the next city over was a round-faced, sweet looking woman, and she looked at them with a genuine apology in her eyes. "There's nothing else I can do at the moment."

Teiwa and At'lokias exchanged concerned looks. How was it possible that there was nothing wrong with her, if she'd been in contact with forbidden magic—not that the medic seemed to believe it—and was now unconscious? That she could stay overnight was a relief, but Teiwa couldn't shake the image of the man at the festival from her mind. Had it happened instantly to him? It took them hours to get to the city from where it happened, despite their fast pace and the fact they didn't stop to rest at all, and Urdara hadn't shown any signs of waking up the entire time.

"So she's not in danger? There's no way she'll die overnight, right?"

The woman gave her a sympathetic smile and placed a hand on her shoulder.

"I can't imagine a reason for that to happen. She's fine. You can go see her if that will make you feel better."

"Ma'am, if I may... Can I stay in the room with her tonight?" she asked. The medic hesitated.

"We're just very worried about her. I promise we don't want any trouble," At'lokias added. "Please."

"I suppose it's fine, but I can't spare any beds. You'll simply have to sleep on the chairs tonight."

"Yes, that's perfect, thank you." Teiwa took the medic's hands in her own and squeezed them. The woman gave her a weak smile. Teiwa looked at At'lokias and opened her mouth to speak, but he didn't give her a chance.

"If you're staying, then I'll stay too."

"What? No, you should go back to the inn! Or... To find an inn, that is." She cringed. They'd come directly to the hospital, and given the late hour, it was possible there simply was nowhere open that would take them in either way.

"I'm not leaving you alone here. If you want to stay, then I'll stay with you."

She wanted to argue, but decided against it. If she convinced him and he couldn't find a place to sleep, she'd essentially be telling him to sleep outside while she stayed with Urdara.

The doctor laughed. "All right then, but I'll need you both to behave. This is still a hospital, all right?"

She winked at the two, and while Teiwa clearly didn't catch her drift, At'lokias did. He almost regretted saying he'd be staying. Almost.

⁂

"Here, you'll catch a cold," he said as he wrapped a blanket around her. He'd taken it out of his bag, and she watched in wonder how it really did fit in without making any volume. If it had been a normal travel bag, it would have been impossible to bring it along. She pulled on one of its sides to wrap herself tighter as he rummaged through his bag. He pulled out an apple and presented it to her, but she shook her head. He shrugged and took a bite.

"Don't you have a blanket for you in there as well?" Teiwa pulled her legs up, hugged them and rested her head on her knees.

"I don't really get cold, remember? I'm always—"

"Warm, right. I remember," she nodded.

Silence fell over them for a time.

"Hey, uh," he started, hesitant. "I just wanted to say thank you."

She raised an eyebrow at him. When she didn't speak, he continued.

"You know. For forgiving me."

She chuckled. "That? I'd actually forgiven you years ago." She looked down with a smile. "It hurt, sure, but I always knew you had a good reason for it."

They sat in silence again for a moment before she perked up. "Oh, you'll like this!" She pulled the chain around her neck free of her dress and held it up for him to see. He reached out and held it in his hand, though she hadn't taken it off so he could only get so close to look. It was a golden chain with a precious stone pendant in a teardrop shape. Despite the somewhat dim light of the room, he could still tell it was aqua colored. He looked up at her and, noticing their proximity, let go of the necklace and jumped back into his chair. She took it back in her hands, still smiling.

"I can't believe you kept that." He looked away from her.

"Kept it?" she chuckled, "I wear it every day. I have done so ever since you gave it to me."

"You have?"

"Of course. It's a gift from a precious friend," she said.

Though his heart beat so fast that it hurt, that night he slept happy.

When morning came, the two were asleep on their chairs. Teiwa had dragged hers close to his and they leaned against each other in their sleep. As the sun came in through the slight opening in the curtains, Urdara woke up, sat up in bed and looked around her, yawning. She did not recognize the room, and she wasn't sure if the sight of two familiar faces was reassuring or somewhat infuriating. As he awakened, At'lokias stirred slightly, which in turn caused Teiwa to wake up as well. The two looked at each other, but as she was about to smile and tell him good morning, he jumped back, causing her to nearly fall over. Urdara snickered at the scene.

"Ah, sorry about that." He rubbed the back of his neck as he spoke. "I got caught off guard."

She just laughed in response. Then, suddenly aware of her friend's consciousness, she turned to face her excitedly. Urdara lifted a hand in greeting and Teiwa immediately moved to check on her. At'lokias sat back on his chair and watched with a smile.

"Are you all right? Does it hurt anywhere? I was so worried about you!"

"I'm fine, it doesn't really hurt anywhere." Urdara shrugged. "I'm still a little tired though."

"Amazing, considering how long you've been sleeping," At'lokias grinned at her, arms crossed behind his head. She threw her pillow at him, but missed. "And now you have no pillow."

Teiwa clearly wanted to laugh, but did her best to look serious as she spoke.

"Now, now, no fighting, you two! Loki, the medic said we had to behave, remember?"

"Yeah, that's really not what she meant. But sure. So, Dara, are you feeling better then? Can we leave?"

She shrugged and pulled the covers off her to get out of bed, but froze when she saw her feet. Teiwa stared wide eyed as well, and At'lokias stood up from his chair to get a closer look. The entire sole of her right foot was covered in what appeared to be a large birthmark, which spread towards the back of her feet in what looked like tendrils. The sole of her left foot was also covered by the strange mark, though it did not seem to be spreading anywhere. The three stared at her feet for a good while, dumbfounded. She wiggled her toes tentatively, but they seemed fine.

"I may be misremembering," At'lokias began, since no one was saying anything. "But I think that wasn't there before."

Urdara and Teiwa both shook their heads. Teiwa reached out and poked one of her feet.

"Does it hurt?"

"Not really? Feels a bit tingly." She eyed her feet suspiciously, still wiggling her toes.

At'lokias stroked his chin in thought. "You know, I think this foot was the one that touched the ground first when you jumped over the tree yesterday." He pointed to her right foot.

She bobbed her head to the sides, somewhat agreeing with him. She didn't like the feeling of doing so. Teiwa grabbed her by the hands and led her out of the bed carefully.

"How about now, does it hurt?" Teiwa said as she watched her movements.

"Still no. It's really just this... weird feeling. Feels a little numb maybe? But it doesn't hurt at all."

Now convinced her friend was fine, Teiwa smacked the back of her head.

"This is why you should listen when someone warns you of danger!"

Urdara looked scandalized and smacked her in return. At'lokias took a step back, before deciding to just go and pick up the bags from the floor.

"Well, if you're all right, and I really don't think the medics here will know what to do about that, I suggest we be on our way," he said, folded Teiwa's blanket and fit it back into the bag.

Together, the three left the hospital.

6

DECISIONS

"Now what?" Urdara crossed her arms in front of her chest as they walked.

"I suppose we find an inn," At'lokias replied. "It's probably best to make sure you're really all right before we continue traveling. I'm still not convinced it's nothing."

Teiwa nodded. "I agree, we shouldn't take any chances. And if anything feels wrong at all, you tell us, all right?"

"Does traveling with him count?" Urdara grinned. At'lokias rolled his eyes. Teiwa smacked her arm.

"You don't have to defend me," At'lokias laughed at the scene. "I don't mind." He raised his arms and entwined his fingers behind his neck.

Urdara raised an eyebrow at him and poked his exposed ribs. "Is this in style in this city by any chance?"

At'lokias flinched as she poked him. He lifted an arm again, careful not to let her near his ribs, and looked down at his shirt. "I hadn't noticed this hole."

"It probably happened when you were getting Urdara out of the area with the forbidden magic yesterday." Teiwa leaned over to see, but as she was on the wrong side, she failed.

"When he what?" Urdara's head snapped to Teiwa.

"You're right," he replied. "We were so worried, I didn't even notice it. Guess I'll need a new shirt."

"When he what?!" Urdara asked again to no avail.

"Don't you have any others in your bag?" Teiwa asked.

"Will you judge me if I say the majority of them are ripped in one place or another?" he replied.

"I will," Urdara said.

He rolled his eyes dramatically. "Come on, I'll just get some new clothes and we can go find an inn after."

He looked around and assessed their surroundings, then picked a direction and led them down the street. They walked down various narrow paths, winding and confusing to them, but not to him. Eventually, after passing by what seemed to be numerous residences, they came out in a street that carried a few shops. He went straight for a small, simple looking one and opened the door for them.

The shop was as small on the inside as it looked from the outside, and fabrics filled the shelves that lined the walls on both sides. Before them, there were a simple counter and a young woman who didn't notice them come in. She had a book before her and read attentively. At'lokias walked up to her and knocked on her head as if it were a door. Teiwa and Urdara's eyes widened.

The young woman jumped and looked up at him. The angry expression on her face was quickly replaced by recognition, then joy, and she rushed around the counter to pull him into a hug. As she pulled away, he signed something to her and raised his arm to show the hole in his shirt. She looked at it, horrified, and smacked the back of his head. He laughed.

"Just wait until I tell her about the other shirts." He smirked back at his friends.

His gesture caught her attention and she looked over his shoulder at them, then smacked him again.

"Why didn't you tell me you had company?" she signed to him.

"I was going to!" he signed back. "Come here." He wrapped an arm around her shoulder and led her to the others. "These are Teiwa and Urdara," he signed to her, pointing to each one before he spelled out their names.

Her eyes widened. "Teiwa?" she signed back.

He made a face. "Yes, anyway." He turned to face the two again. "Ladies, this is Yanna. She and her mother are the best seamstresses in town," he said, signing at the same time so she wouldn't miss a word.

"It's a pleasure to meet you," Urdara signed to her and she beamed up.

"What, since when do you know sign language?" At'lokias asked.

"Since knowing multiple languages is good for business." She shrugged. "Why, since when do you know it?"

Teiwa frowned. "Since he was eight, remember? Captain Goras taught him so he could talk to the mermaids."

"Talk or flirt?" Urdara grinned, signing it along.

"Talk." He glared at her.

Yanna laughed. She motioned for them to come closer to the counter. They obeyed and as At'lokias approached, she grabbed him by the shoulder and pulled down. He yelped and she pulled on the back of his shirt until it came off and hit him with it. He screamed the entire time, but he was in no position to sign, though it wouldn't have helped.

"What's happening?" Teiwa looked to Urdara, concerned.

At'lokias yelped again as Yanna hit him with his shirt some more.

Urdara snickered. "Who cares? This is great."

Yanna collected the other shirts he produced from his bag and hurried with them to the back room. At'lokias straightened and sighed.

They gasped.

His back was marked with three long scars, running from one of his shoulders down and across his back. They took up the majority of his torso. He heard their reaction and tried to look at his back to see what the matter was. "Oh."

"What in the world happened to you?" Teiwa rushed to him and put her hands on his scars. He felt a cold shiver run up his back and shuddered. She grimaced. "Oh, sorry."

"It looks worse than it is." He shrugged and turned back to face them.

Urdara leaned back against a chair and watched him with a smirk. He felt the urge to cover himself with one of the fabrics from the shelves.

"So," she said as she tilted her head forward at him, "what caused those?"

"Bar fight," he replied, deadpan.

They both opened their mouths, but didn't have time to speak.

"I thought you'd said you fell down the stairs," a woman said as she came out of the back room.

"Yes, during a bar fight." At'lokias shrugged.

"Don't listen to him." She grinned at the two younger women. "He gives a different answer every time. Hello, I'm Aymar, Yanna's mother. It's a pleasure to meet friends of Loki's."

"It's our pleasure." Teiwa smiled and offered the woman her hand to shake. "I'm Teiwa, and this is Urdara."

"Yes, my daughter told me, you're his childhood friends. Say, can we make you two anything? I'd be happy to. Happier than we are to make him new shirts yet again." She glared at him, but he was unaffected.

"Oh, no, we're fine." Teiwa shook her hands before her. Urdara nodded in agreement. Teiwa looked over at At'lokias and the realization that his torso was still exposed hit her. Heat made its way to her face, ears and chest and she choked on air. She looked to the ceiling as she spoke. "Though, if it's not much to ask, do you perhaps have something Loki can wear for now?"

"Why cover him?" Urdara asked. "It's a nice view."

At'lokias couldn't tell if he should be pleased or uncomfortable. In his doubt, he flicked a finger in Urdara's direction and shot her a sheepish smile. She winked and laughed when his smile disappeared.

❧ ❧

"You know, figuring out a plan is probably not the worst idea," At'lokias said as he fished in his bag for something. They'd found an inn and gotten themselves two rooms, but were all sitting in the same one while they discussed their journey. "Not that I don't enjoy traveling blindly."

"I'm sorry about that, by the way," Teiwa said. "I'm sure this is the worst job you could have possibly gotten, not knowing where we're going or for how long..."

"It's fine." He shrugged. "I told the boss I had a long-term job so I didn't know when I'd be back. Which means I'm all yours." He winked at her.

She smiled. Urdara groaned.

"If we're heading northwest though, we should probably take... One second." He produced the map from his bag and spread it out on the desk before him. "Here. This road should be the fastest this time of year. That said—"

Urdara stood from the bed she'd been sitting on to lean over and look at the map. "Does that go through Riverhill? I've heard there was a storm there just the other day, it's no good."

He frowned at her. "When did you hear that? We've just been to the seamstresses and back here."

"I could have heard it on the way, you don't know." She crossed her arms and huffed.

Teiwa tilted her head to the side. She hadn't heard anything, herself, but Urdara was certainly more observant than she was. Still, she trusted At'lokias' judgment too.

"All right, easy. I can go downstairs and ask if anyone has heard anything. But what I was going to say is, do we know what we're going to do once we're there?"

Urdara and At'lokias both turned to look at Teiwa on the bed. She squirmed under their gaze, hands wiggling her dress mindlessly. "Uhm, well... I..."

"Are you saying you don't have a plan at all for once you reach Yrathea?" Urdara glared at her.

"I was hoping she would tell me what she needs me to do once I'm there!"

"That's the dumbest plan possible!" Urdara threw her hands up. "You can't just get there completely unprepared and hope for the best. Do we even know if there is anything that can be done against forbidden magic?"

Teiwa shook her head.

"You're unbelievable," Urdara snarled.

"If we don't have a plan for that, may I offer a suggestion?" At'lokias pinched his nose bridge and sighed. "The library at Elwind is the biggest in the country. If there's anywhere we'll find information about forbidden magic, it's there."

Urdara's head snapped back to him. "Elwind? That's south! It'll take us completely off course!"

"Do we even have a course, though? It's not like we know where our destination is. Might as well know we're prepared, at least." He shrugged.

Teiwa worried her lower lip as she thought. Before her, At'lokias and Urdara continued to argue, but she didn't hear a word. They had a point. She'd just been aimlessly following her instincts without a plan. She had no idea what she would do once she found Yrathea and she didn't even know if it really was possible to save her, especially on her own. Shame made heat creep up her face and ears. She was hardly worthy of having been chosen.

"Fine!" Urdara threw her arms up and yelled. "Have it your way!" The outburst was enough to pull Teiwa from her thoughts.

At'lokias sighed deeply, then turned to Teiwa. "So, what do you think?"

She wriggled her skirt some more. "I think... We pay Elwind a visit."

7
VISIT

It was a quiet day and Ashtari was in her room, pregnant with what would be her first and only child.

"May we come in?"

The voice came from the door and pulled Ashtari from her daydreaming. It was Numa, with a tiny Balri hiding behind her skirt. He clung to her for dear life and she laughed.

"Sorry, he was dying to come see his auntie, but now that we're here, it looks like he's a bit nervous. Come on, don't you wanna say hi to auntie Ashtari and your little cousin?" she prompted gently. He nodded. "Well, go ahead."

The small boy took a tentative step forward and waved a tiny hand at his aunt. She smiled and spread her arms in invitation. He looked over to his mother and when she nodded, walked over to his aunt.

It was late in Ashtari's pregnancy, a long wait of several months bedridden, after three previous attempts at making her dream of motherhood come true. This was her very last chance, one even her fellow medics advised against, and she couldn't risk standing up to greet them. Her stomach was large and heavy with the child she'd waited so long for and as the little boy came closer, she rested a hand on it and patted his head with the other.

"Do you want to feel them?" She tilted her head to the side, a gentle and patient smile gracing her features. His face lit up.

"May I, auntie?"

"Of course, my love. Go on."

He put his hands on her stomach and stared in amazement. For the first months of her pregnancy, he wasn't allowed to visit. She needed to rest and her visits were limited to only her attendants and her sister in law. She'd missed her nephew dearly, and to see his expression brought her great joy. She stroked his short, blonde hair and sighed dreamily, thinking of the child she too would soon have to call her own.

"Auntie, does he kick? Mama says babies kick inside their mama's bellies sometimes. Does he?"

He. She didn't blame the boy for the certainty of her child's gender. In reality, she was the only one unconvinced. There was a long line of male firstborns in her husband's family, but this was her fourth pregnancy, and she was thrilled to have a baby, boy or not. She knew they would all love the child no matter what, but it was amusing how everyone treated it as fact. They didn't even have a name picked, should it be a girl. For a boy, they'd chosen Teiwal. It was the name of her husband's late older brother, the reason they'd met all those years ago.

She'd have given that name to the first child she came to expect, if not out of respect for Numa's grief. The second and third pregnancies too came to have other names. It was only at her fourth that she was given Numa's blessings to use the name. She'd say it was the name that protected this child, some sort of influence from the beyond, but in reality her belief was different. She'd prayed to Death every time she became pregnant before—a custom common to both her culture and her husband's—so that should the pregnancy not come to term, the child would be safely taken into the afterlife by the god. But after praying and having it happen three times, she decided to change things. Go against the current, in a way. And so she prayed to Life, that she may protect the life growing inside of her and keep it safe until it was time to meet this world, and she prayed to Chaos, that no misfortune befall her and her family so that she may carry to term. So far, it seemed to be working. And so, against all customs again, she planned on asking the two goddesses—rather than one—for her child's protection upon their birth.

The expectant expression in the eyes of the boy before her brought her back to the present.

"They do. Very hard, too. It's a strong one, this cousin of yours." She grinned.

"Oohh." His expression was still one of wonder. He put his ear on her stomach and stroked it gently. "Please stay strong and come out soon, cousin! I can't wait to meet you. I love you!" He kissed her stomach and ran back to his mother. She giggled.

"I'm sure they're excited to meet you, too."

Numa stroked his head as he reached her. "Did you get to say what you wanted to your auntie and your cousin?"

"Yes, Mama."

"Good, then go wait for me downstairs, will you? I'll be right there."

He nodded vigorously and ran down the hallway, then stopped, turned around and ran back into the room. "Bye auntie, bye baby cousin! I love you!"

Ashtari chuckled and waved at him before he left again.

Numa's visit didn't take long. The two saw each other often enough, and Ashtari had to rest as much as possible. But the two women were very similar and they'd bonded instantly like sisters from the moment she came into the family. Ashtari had always been grateful to them all for accepting her so readily. Numa and her parents had all been welcoming and it was a comfort after losing the family she used to have. She'd sworn to always be good to them and make sure they never came to regret taking her in. So far so good, and now with a child on the way, her position in the family seemed even stronger.

She only wished her parents in law had been able to live to see that day. How thrilled they would have been to see their youngest son become a father, himself. It was in their honor, too, that she insisted so much on having a child despite all adversities. Her dream of being a mother came first, of course, but to give the two the grandchild they deserved was a close second. If only she'd been able to give them multiple grandchildren, her happiness would have been complete.

The baby kicked inside her belly and she chuckled. "Sorry," she whispered to her stomach, as if the child was protesting over her thoughts. "You know A'mma loves you more than anything, right? I just wish you could grow up with brothers, that's all. But that was an unfair thought to have. My happiness is complete with you, so please just be born healthy."

Unbeknown to her, another figure watched the future mother from the side of the bed. A woman hummed to herself as her invisible hand stroked Ashtari's stomach without really touching it.

"Don't worry," she said with a wide smile, "she will be."

8

STALKER

"Before we go, there's something I want to do," Urdara declared.

Her mood seemed sour enough that Teiwa was tempted to just say yes without asking what it was, but At'lokias didn't give her that chance.

"What's that?"

"Gotta do a favor for someone."

He raised an eyebrow. She hardly seemed the kind to be concerned about others, and if they'd passed by someone she knew, shouldn't she have told them as much? It wouldn't make sense that she'd be hiding their journey either. Or did it? Even if she didn't want to be open about her reasons for traveling, she could always claim it was a business trip.

"Sure, but who is it?" he asked.

"I don't know them yet." She shrugged. "But they need a favor, and I'm going to help them out."

At'lokias and Teiwa both stared at her in shock. To assume she was concerned about someone she knew was one thing, and even then it seemed a stretch, but this was beyond weird. She didn't appear to think so, however, given she offered them no further explanation.

"I think I speak for us both when I say we're going to need more information than that," At'lokias said, and Teiwa nodded in agreement.

Urdara rolled her eyes. "It's this thing I do. It's kind of like a hobby, all right? Think of it as a secondary business. I find someone in need of help, and I help them out. In exchange, they owe me a favor. I don't know when or even if I'll ever call it, but I always make sure it's something they can do. You'd be surprised how big of a network I've set up doing this already."

"So why do you do that, exactly?" he asked.

"Because then they owe me, weren't you listening? It's fun to get people to be grateful and indebted to you, it makes you feel powerful. You should try it sometime. Besides, it can come quite in handy at times, too."

Now that seemed more like her type of thing. He sighed. It seemed a very inappropriate reason for helping others, but at least she was doing it. It seemed unfair to deny someone the assistance they need just because one's motivations are questionable.

"Just one last question, but how do you know of this person in need of help?" Teiwa piped in.

"I heard it on the way here, just like I heard about the storm. Just because your head is always in the clouds doesn't mean mine has to be as well. Or I guess I might say your head is always in the leaves, instead." She snorted.

Teiwa made a face, but decided not to argue. At least she seemed to be in a better mood, even if that meant being mean. Still, she heard enough teasing about her magical affinity back at home from near strangers. It would be nice to have a break from it from a friend. But surely it was meant in jest, just friendly banter. She took a deep breath and tried to keep herself from being affected by it.

"Then we'll help you help that person! Right, Loki?" She smiled at him.

"We'll what? Us? Uh, right. I guess. Sure." He wanted to punch himself. He had no intention of joining Urdara's weird ego club, but it wasn't her asking, it was Teiwa. And she was smiling at him. And she was so pretty when she smiled. Or at any other moment. It was almost infuriating. Not that she was pretty, but how much of an idiot he clearly was.

Urdara frowned and watched them for a moment, arms crossed. "Very well, you two can be my assistants for today."

Great.

❧❧❧❧❧❧ ❧❧❧❧❧❧

When they found the young woman Urdara had overheard, she was jumpy and shaking, constantly looking from side to side. They approached her carefully, and yet she still yelped when they called out to her.

"I'm so sorry," she said. "I... I haven't been well. Please forgive me. May I help you?"

"Actually," Urdara said with a grin, "it's us that are here to help you."

"Huh?"

She swiftly moved an arm over the young woman's shoulder and led her to the side as she explained her hobby to her, though she made a point not to use that word. Business sounded far more professional. Teiwa and At'lokias exchanged glances as they waited. Urdara and the young woman spoke for a time before she brought her back to them.

"So, this is Minna," Urdara said.

"Mirra."

"Or that. And she believes she's being followed. I told her we're going to find out by whom and put an end to it."

At'lokias raised an eyebrow. "And how exactly are we going to go about doing that?"

"Ironically enough, we're going to follow her around until we find who's following her around."

Teiwa opened her mouth to speak, but said nothing. At'lokias pursed his lips.

"Are you comfortable with that, Mirra?" he asked.

"Y-yes, I suppose it's fine, so long as I know it's just you three making sure I'm safe and helping me get to the end of this."

He looked to Teiwa and found she was already looking at him. She shrugged and he did the same.

"Then I guess let's get to it," he said.

The three of them spent the entire day following Mirra from a distance. In order to better observe her surroundings, they split up and each followed from one direction. For the majority of the day, nothing seemed out of the ordinary and any people who happened to be in more than one place she'd been to seemed to have done it out of a coincidence rather than malice.

She carried on with her chores as usual. Wherever she went, merchants looked at her with sympathy, and a touch of incredibility. Teiwa knew that look all too well. She'd gotten it many times over the years from people who only claimed to believe her when she spoke of her gift. In reality, it was clear from the way they spoke to her—and behind her back when they thought she couldn't hear—and looked at her that the only thing they believed was that she was insane.

"It's infuriating, isn't it?" The voice came from behind her and Teiwa jumped. A figure moved from a shady, narrow street between buildings to stand by her side. They wore a cloak that hid their face. Absolutely suspicious, she decided.

When she said nothing, they continued. "This isn't the first time this happens, you know. She's well known around these parts for lying, or for being insane. Depends on who you ask."

She clearly wasn't lying, Teiwa thought, if this strange person—a man judging by the voice—really was following her around. And if he wasn't, then what was he doing hiding in dark alleyways and commenting on her? Yet something intrigued her. She hadn't commented on her thoughts at all. How did he know she was paying attention to the way they looked at her, specifically? To any normal observer, she would just be watching a normal daily scene. She turned to look at the man, but he turned his face away from her. Definitely suspicious. She wondered if she could indicate his presence to the others without him noticing.

"She's always been the odd girl around these parts. She'd sense things, predict things. People couldn't understand, so they'd ignore her warnings and later claim she didn't really predict anything; that it was obvious or that she only spoke of it after it happened and said she'd done it before. It was the only way they could go about their lives. Otherwise they'd have to question everything. How was it possible that she knew? I was like them too, once."

She listened closely to every word he said, but her eyes were trained on Urdara and At'lokias nearby. They were focused on Mirra, not her. Besides, the scene probably didn't seem too off to them, from where they stood. The man wasn't close enough to her that they'd seem to be interacting, and there were others not too far from where they stood. It could very well be someone waiting for an acquaintance. If only she could signal to them that it was not the case, that she needed them to come over. Would he notice? Would he run?

She swallowed. "What changed?"

"It was a few weeks ago. I caught a fish in the creek nearby, and Mirra saw me coming home with it. She told me not to eat it. Said there was something off about it. I thought that was ridiculous. It looked perfectly normal to me, and besides, everyone knows Mirra isn't to be believed."

"But she was right." Teiwa nodded.

"I don't know how, but I can't find any other explanation. That night, I felt pain like I'd never felt before. When I woke up the next morning, I was... Different. I've been following her. I want to ask how to fix this, but I can't bring myself to show this face to her. I should have listened. We all should have listened. What's coming next? Who's going to suffer like me? I need to warn others, but how can I do that when I look like this?"

Teiwa knitted her brows at that and turned to face him. He was looking directly at her and pulled back his hood.

His face looked melted.

She fell down with a scream. People around her turned to look. Urdara and At'lokias rushed from their own spots, but were stopped by the commotion that quickly formed around them. Mirra turned to look and fainted. A man next to her caught her before she hit the ground.

The man tried to cover his face again, but it was too late. People had seen him and were closing in on them from all sides, some screaming in fear, others in anger, others simply confused. Seeing no other way out of it, he removed his hood again.

In the sun, Teiwa could see his hands glistened. A drop of a liquid fell off. Her eyes widened. He *was* melting.

"She was right!" the man screamed. "She's been right all along! You have to believe her!"

The clouds that covered the sun moved so that a ray hit him directly. He let out an inhuman shriek as his skin liquified more and more where the sun hit, until pieces of his face and hands were falling to the ground.

The people around them screamed and ran in all directions. At'lokias picked up a child nearby so she wouldn't be stepped on in the commotion. Urdara held on to a pole to keep herself from being dragged by the crowd.

Teiwa's eyes brimmed with tears as she watched the man fall apart before her.

❧❧❧❧❧ ❧❧❧❧❧

"Are you sure you'll be all right?" the woman asked as she handed Teiwa a cup of tea.

Despite the heat, she shuddered under the blanket that At'lokias had placed around her shoulders. She nodded weakly. Beside her, Mirra clung to a cup of her own, eyes watery. The young man who had held her when she collapsed stood beside them, worried.

"I can't believe he died like that." Mirra said. "I don't understand, it's simply impossible."

"It's possible." Teiwa said as she stared at the floor before her.

Her mind raced back to the man at the festival. He asked her to help him, and she never even knew his name. If what the nurse told her was true, she had no reason to think the events of the day any less possible. Somehow, though, this felt worse. The way he screamed as he came undone before her, the way his entire body fell apart little by little until it was all an indistinct mass on the ground. How could that ever have been a person? Did he feel it until the very end?

She didn't know how to stop the images in her mind. Among them, only one rational thought: she had to save Yrathea.

9

RECONCILIATION

The road to Elwind was long and though Urdara was not pleased, there was no way to avoid camping. At'lokias helped make a fire and the fallen logs they found nearby made for good benches, but none of them looked forward to night time. For Urdara, because it meant sleeping on the ground. For Teiwa and At'lokias, because it meant listening to Urdara's complaints about it. She'd been nice enough for the days following the events in that square, though she was often away at night time, but now that Teiwa had had time to recover from it, she was back to her usual self.

They hadn't been walking for long when he noticed Teiwa wasn't wearing any shoes.

"What are you doing?" he asked.

She cocked her head to the side, confused.

"Your shoes," he clarified, "you're not wearing them."

"Oh! Right. I don't like it. This way, I can feel all the roots along the way. It doesn't hurt, don't worry. I'll make sure to put them on again if I feel the need to."

He raised an eyebrow, but decided not to question. It was normal of her to choose to go barefoot, but it was unusual to have anyone travel on an actual road that way. Although usual was never a word he'd have used to refer to her, anyway.

They'd been able to follow the river, which meant easy access to clean water and fishing opportunities. One day, At'lokias called them over to the water to show them how to catch dinner.

"This," he said as he held up the makeshift spear up for them to see, "is a spear. Sort of. You want to focus before you throw it, it's not just tossing it into the water. You have to really put your mind to it. Aim, focus, and throw. Who wants to try?"

"That's a hard pass," Urdara said from the rock she'd found to sit on.

"I do!" Teiwa waddled over to where he was, holding the skirt of her dress up as she did.

At'lokias tried not to laugh. "That's not gonna work. How are you going to throw the spear if your hands are busy holding your clothes? Either tie it up, or don't worry about it and I'll dry it for you later."

"Dry it for me?"

He shrugged. "With magic. I do it often, don't worry. I won't burn you, or your clothes."

She thought for a moment and let go of her dress. She tried to ignore how her skirt clung to her legs as it floated around her and picked a fish to focus on. He handed her the spear.

"When you feel you're ready, don't hesitate. Really go for it." He nodded at a fish swimming by.

She held the spear with both hands and moved her shoulders in antici-pation. He held back another laugh. Urdara didn't.

"I can't focus with you laughing," Teiwa protested.

"I can't not laugh with you fishing." Urdara grinned.

Teiwa tried to ignore her friend. She closed her eyes and took a deep breath. She could feel the water running past her, cold and refreshing. She felt the fish passing by her legs. The breeze on her face. She opened her eyes, chose a fish, and lunged at it.

When At'lokias pulled her out of the water, Urdara was hysterical.

"I think you went for it a little too much." He patted her back as she coughed out water. He took the spear from her hands and pushed her gently towards the land. "How about you wait over there? I'll catch us dinner and get you dried in a bit."

She sat beside Urdara and huffed.

It didn't take long for At'lokias to catch enough fish for the three of them. He tossed each one to the ground by their feet as he caught them, and shot them a triumphant grin as he did. Urdara rolled her eyes dramatically. Teiwa just pouted.

"And this," he said as he started walking towards the river bank, "is how you catch fish."

He tripped.

Urdara nearly fell off the rock with laughter.

❧❧❧❧❧❧ ❧❧❧❧❧❧

"All right," a very muddy At'lokias dusted off his hands, the only reasonably clean part of him. "I've prepared the fish and dried Tei. Now can I trust you two to watch them roast while I clean myself?"

They both nodded, though Urdara did so with a snicker. His eyes narrowed at her.

"I'll be right back, then."

He'd already taken off his clothes and walked into the river to wash himself when he heard someone clearing their throat and jumped, hands moving to cover himself instinctively.

"So anyway." Urdara grinned.

"What. What are you... What is wrong with you? I'm naked here!"

"I'm not blind, you know. Come on, we used to bathe together all the time as kids, it's not that big of a deal. You don't have anything I haven't seen already." She shrugged.

His eyes narrowed and he lowered himself further into the water. "What do you want?"

She shifted uncomfortably and he raised an eyebrow at the display. It was unlike her.

"Would you believe it if I said I just wanted to watch you squirm?"

He stared at her, expressionless. "No. I mean, yes. But no."

She stared back. They stayed that way for an uncomfortable amount of time, though he would argue any amount of time would be uncomfortable under those circumstances. It may not be what brought her there, but he surely was squirming, if only on the inside.

"Fine!" she declared, suddenly angry. "I wanted to come here to say... Thank you."

He frowned. "For what?"

"Teiwa told me you saved me back there on the road to the city, and then carried me all the way to the hospital without stopping to rest."

"To be fair, she didn't get to stop to rest either." He shrugged.

"Did she carry me?"

"No."

"Then I don't care."

He snorted a laugh. She held back the urge to do the same.

"Well, you're welcome. Though there was no need to thank me," he said.

"Yes, there was. You saved my life, probably, maybe. Perhaps. And besides, I know I haven't exactly been very nice to you so far."

He shrugged. "You have your reasons."

"I do, but I might be going a little overkill with it. I'll try to do better. But not too much. Don't get your hopes up."

"I promise I will manage my expectations accordingly."

Urdara nodded and jumped off the rock she'd sat on. She began to walk back towards the camp, then stopped and turned back to him. He'd started letting his hands down, but put them back in front of him immediately. She snorted.

"By the way, if you're ever interested..."

"I'm really, really not."

She shrugged. "It was worth a shot."

Teiwa perked up as Urdara walked back into the camp. Then she frowned. "Didn't you head out in that direction?" She pointed away from the river.

"Did I? Huh, how weird." Urdara feigned surprise and sat by the fire. "Is the fish ready?"

Teiwa knew better than to press her, so she decided to just let it go. The fish was about ready and she turned the sticks around so they would roast evenly. At'lokias joined them not long after, and by then it was good enough to eat. Teiwa considered again the idea of asking them about it, but something about the way Urdara grinned at At'lokias and he glared at her gave her pause. Maybe it was better to just not know.

"So," Urdara started as she grabbed one of the sticks, "Tei. How's life?"

"What do you mean?" Teiwa raised an eyebrow at the question. As if they hadn't been together the past several days already. At'lokias grabbed a stick and blew on it. He took a bite.

"Oh you know. Just wondering about how you've been in all those years we were apart. Are you seeing anyone, perhaps?" She grinned, her eyes directed at At'lokias. He choked.

"Too hot," he said in an attempt to justify it.

Teiwa frowned. "That's... Well, no, I'm not. I was, before, but it's over now. You remember Trex, right?"

At'lokias was glad he hadn't taken another bite yet. Trex? Of all people? What could she have possibly seen in that unpleasant, good for nothing guard wannabe? He couldn't think of a worse option, though he supposed there weren't many options he would have been happy with. Urdara, meanwhile, started laughing.

"No, you must be kidding me. Trex? I never expected him to have any interest in you."

Ouch.

"Well, he did, for a few years. And then he didn't anymore, and I'd rather not talk about that." Teiwa fiddled with her skirt. She still hadn't taken a stick. Urdara noticed it was starting to burn and handed it to her, unaffected.

At'lokias pursed his lips. He didn't know what to say to that, but even if he was happy she wasn't with that guy anymore, he also didn't like seeing her sad. She was clearly still upset over whatever had happened, and that was just one more reason to dislike the guy.

"You know, you shouldn't be upset about that guy. I mean, his name is Trex, for gods' sake. Like that dragon t'rex, with the teeny tiny arms," Urdara said, holding her elbows close to her chest and shaking her hands in a mimicry of the dragon.

"That's so mean!" Teiwa protested.

"What, you're gonna defend him? Please."

"What about you, Dara?" At'lokias asked loudly, unsure what to do to redirect the conversation away from Teiwa's failed relationship and the fact that yes, Trex's name was indeed ridiculous.

"Oh, I don't do the romance thing," she said with a shrug. "I only do the fun thing. Which I hear is your case, too."

Teiwa looked up from her fish with one eyebrow raised. He regretted having opened his mouth.

"What do you mean you hear?" His eyes narrowed.

"What can I say, you have a reputation and I've heard a thing or two when I was out having said fun."

"You mean to say people just randomly talk about my love life to strangers?"

"I mean to say I snooped around and people will talk about just about anything with the right encouragement." She shot him a grin he felt was almost malicious.

Not for the first time that day, he felt himself squirming internally under her gaze. The Urdara he'd known as a child was smart, witty, and nosy, sure, but this was different. He was torn between wondering what happened during those years, and being too uncomfortable to care.

They ate in silence for a moment before Urdara broke it again. Of course.

"Trex the ex," she snorted.

He grabbed a stick from the ground and threw it at her head.

<hr>

The sun rose and hit Teiwa's face, and she squeezed her eyes closed in an attempt to escape it, but the angle was just so that she couldn't. She groaned and sat up. Urdara still slept soundly, but At'lokias was nowhere to be found. His blanket was gone, as was his bag. She thought back about Urdara's accusations that he would leave them in the middle of nowhere, but shook her head to rid herself of the thought. No matter what he'd done back then, he would never do such a thing. She was sure of it. And especially after saving Urdara, and staying all night with them at the hospital. She stood and went to look for him.

She found him by the river, shaving. "Loki?" she asked, hesitant.

He jumped and dropped the razor in the river. "Gods! What happened?"

"Oh, I'm sorry! I just... I woke up and you weren't at the camp, so I came looking for you. Are you... Shaving?"

He turned to look at her with pursed lips and a half shaved beard. "I was. Believe it or not, I don't keep this look just by sheer will. But I guess that's it for my blade." He turned back to the river and stuck his hand in to look for it. It was gone.

She grimaced. "I'm sorry, I'll buy you a new one in the next city over."

"It's fine. I'll improvise, that's what I do." He grabbed his bag and rummaged through it.

She'd heard him say you'd always find what you're looking for in the bag, but what if you didn't know what you were after? She didn't understand how it was possible for so many things to fit in there with magic, while he still could simply stick his hand in and feel around for what he wanted. The magic of light elves truly made no sense to her.

He took a dagger out of the bag and inspected it for a moment. Teiwa cringed as he shrugged and deemed it suitable. He turned back towards the water with it.

"What are you guys up to?" Urdara's voice came from behind them.

At'lokias jumped. "What is it with you two? Can't you see me by the river without coming to interrupt me?"

"I guess we can't." Urdara messed with a leaf she plucked from a nearby branch. "So, again, what are you guys up to?"

"I'm *trying* to shave," At'lokias sighed. "And Teiwa just came to look for me because I wasn't at the camp."

She raised an eyebrow. "You're trying to shave with a dagger."

"Yes, Urdara, I'm trying to shave with a dagger. I lost my blade. Is that a problem?"

She shrugged. "It's just weird, that's all. Good luck not getting yourself killed." She looked around and when he took the dagger to his neck to continue shaving, she spoke again. "What's for breakfast?"

He took a deep breath and rubbed his eyes with his free hand. "Fruit. Now would you please wait back at the camp? Both of you."

Teiwa nodded apologetically and dragged an unhappy Urdara by the arm as she left. He watched them leave, turned back around and let out a heavy sigh.

The river ran past him and At'lokias watched his reflection in the water, so distorted it was barely there at all. He took the blade to his neck again and this time, without interruptions, he was able to finish shaving.

He dropped the dagger beside him and sat there, staring at the river for a time. His chest ached with a weight he couldn't shake and he held back the scream that threatened to escape him. It wasn't supposed to be this way. They weren't supposed to be on this journey at all. He was supposed to have succeeded. They'd have been safe and sound in their homes, oblivious to the dangers of forbidden magic.

Instead here they were, heading straight towards danger. Urdara had already fallen victim to it once, and it was a wonder she hadn't been injured, though he still worried there may be more consequences than just the odd marks on her feet. He didn't know exactly what had happened to the man at the festival—Teiwa had been oddly vague about it all—but he knew whatever it was, it had gotten him killed. As much as Urdara had been finding pleasure in bothering him, he would never wish harm upon her.

"Can we talk? Now?" he said, his voice low.

Only silence answered him.

He waited, quiet, for a sign, any sign. There was nothing. He pursed his lips and nodded. "I guess not."

10

THE TRIP

Travel from there was easy and straightforward. The road was clear for the most part and with a trail to follow, there was no need to worry about getting lost. The next city was only a few days away, and from there they would catch a caravan to Elwind.

They walked during the day and rested after dark. Trees surrounded them from both sides of their path and they had no clearings nearby, so they resorted to setting up camp on the road. No other travelers passed by them, though At'lokias claimed it was a fairly well-traveled road. From the state of it, Teiwa saw no reason to doubt him.

They sat on the ground and ate their dinner. Dry rations, as they'd strayed from the river now. Urdara made a face, but didn't complain more than a mumble. Teiwa ate with little interest, her attention turned to the trees around them. They were different from the trees she was used to back at home and she found their shapes fascinating, even if she knew her friends would probably not see much of a difference.

"Do you think I can take a little time tomorrow morning to explore the area and see what kind of herbs grow around here?" she asked.

Urdara raised an eyebrow. "It's weeds, they're the same everywhere."

"It's not weeds, it's herbs. With the right ones, I can make all sorts of things."

At'lokias swallowed the piece of bread he'd had in his mouth. "So is that what you do for a living? You're an apothecary?"

She shook her head. "It's just a hobby. I'm still learning from my father to take his place when he retires." Her voice was small and sounded almost defeated.

He frowned. "I thought you didn't want to be chief."

Teiwa just shrugged weakly in response.

Urdara bit off a large chunk of dried meat from her rations. "That's bullshit."

Teiwa looked up at her, confused. "Excuse me?"

"You've never wanted that job, why are you training to take over the position? The Teiwa I knew would have stood up for herself and made clear what she really wanted to do."

Silence hovered over them for too long a moment before Teiwa spoke again.

"Sorry to disappoint," she said.

"That's ridiculous, don't apologize for that! What happened to you? You turned soft and weak while I was gone. I don't like this new you. Where's the old Tei?"

Teiwa caught her gaze and held it, her expression serious, almost angry. "It's hard to stay strong when you're all on your own."

Urdara hesitated for an instant before she took on an angry expression herself. "I was on my own too, and look what I became. I'm strong, I'm smart, I'm powerful and I don't need anyone. You're just looking for an excuse for the fact you were too lazy to fight for yourself."

"Whoa, now," At'lokias interrupted, hands up in a pacifying motion, "let's not get too heated here. It's all right. Tei knows what's best for her. I'm sure she weighed her options before she made that decision and it's not our place to argue it with her."

Urdara grumbled in response and turned to the side to continue her meal facing away from them. Teiwa just stared down at the bread in her hands. At'lokias sighed and placed a hand on her shoulder, which she leaned against slightly, the smallest hint of a smile on her face. For now, that was enough.

When morning came, Urdara didn't protest against Teiwa's request to explore the region. They packed up their things and headed to the wooded area, Teiwa barefoot as was her usual. Just as she'd expected, the place held many herbs she couldn't find on her island and she was thrilled for the opportunity to collect samples and study them. She took out a box from her bag and opened it, revealing a journal and several types of dried herbs underneath. It was neatly organized, with separators in the box to hold different categories of plants, though neither Urdara nor At'lokias could make any sense of what order they were in or what any of it was exactly. She held the journal open and pressed herbs between the pages carefully, a wide smile on her face.

At'lokias watched her and couldn't help but smile, himself. She looked like she belonged in that scene so perfectly. He could understand Urdara's frustration with her the night before, though she could have handled it better. He leaned against a tree and stayed there, content to just see her happy. Urdara fiddled with the flowers in a patch, bored.

"So anyway," she started, her voice disinterested, "we never did finish that conversation about Trex from the other day."

At'lokias looked towards them but didn't say anything. He wasn't fond of the subject, either.

"I think that's because I said I didn't want to talk about it," Teiwa replied, holding up an herb to the light and inspecting it before she pressed it against the sheets of her journal.

"That would explain it. Do you wanna talk about it now? Like, how old were you guys? Was that a recent thing or…?"

Teiwa sighed deeply and turned to face Urdara. She wasn't about to give this up, was she? "I was sixteen and he was seventeen when it started. We were together until a few months ago. People thought we were going to get married, but instead he broke up with me on our anniversary and told me he didn't love me and never had. Happy now?"

Urdara made a face. "No, that's awful. I can see why you didn't want to talk about it, it must have been humiliating."

Teiwa stared at her, lips pursed. "Thanks."

"You shouldn't let him do that to you." Urdara shrugged. "You're way better than that idiot, so you should humiliate him back. That's what I think."

"Thanks?"

Urdara nodded in response, then looked back down at the flowers she'd been fiddling with. "What do you think these are?" She pulled on one and it didn't come off. Lifting an eyebrow, she pulled again, a little harder.

A growl came from the patch and it began to rise slowly. The trio stared, wide eyed, as a flower-covered dragon stood and roared at them. A t'rex dragon.

It stood at roughly knee height compared to them.

"I don't know what to make of this," was all Urdara managed to say before it roared again, more fiercely this time, and the trio ran.

It chased after them, its tiny arms flapping in front of it, but its hind legs strong and its stride much wider than any of them expected. Despite its small stature, its teeth and claws were sharp and they knew better than to risk a confrontation.

"This is the most ridiculous problem I've ever gotten into!" Urdara exclaimed as she ran.

"No, it isn't!" At'lokias replied and pulled her out of the way of a tree.

The three ran through the woods, dodging branches and tree roots to the best of their ability. Teiwa was especially nimble with it and At'lokias cursed his fire affinity for being useless at a time like this. While not a fire dragon itself, the t'rex had very resistant skin and would not be burned easily. If only he could get ahead of it enough to find a weapon in his bag, but the critter was fast, too.

They turned to the left to avoid a particularly large tree and continued running, with the dragon close at their heels. Then Teiwa stopped abruptly. Before her, a small ravine. At'lokias was able to stop right before bumping into her, but Urdara collided with him and he accidentally pushed Teiwa forward, but reached out and pulled her back before she could fall. Doing their best not to waste time, they turned right and continued to run alongside it. The dragon nearly fell into it, but was able to regain its balance and continued the chase.

"It's not going to stop!" Teiwa exclaimed, her breath starting to sound labored.

"What do you suggest we do, then?" Urdara yelled back at her, and from afar, they heard the roar of another dragon. This one sounded louder and filled the trio with dread.

"We need to find shelter!" She screamed back at her friend, looking around her as she ran. "Climb!"

She didn't give them a chance to think before she jumped on the nearest tree and started her climb. At'lokias stopped and helped Urdara start hers before he followed suit. With the three sitting on the tree, the dragon wouldn't be able to reach them. It stopped at the base and started jumping up and down in one last attempt.

"Does that thing never give up? I didn't even pull that hard," Urdara groaned.

"Maybe next time you can ask the plant expert before you go on pulling any flowers. Just. Any flowers." At'lokias said, his breath ragged.

"I'm more concerned about getting it to go away before the bigger one finds us," Teiwa added, leaning forward to look around for what she assumed must be one of the parents of the dragon that was after them.

The trio sat and waited for a time, no one able to come up with a plan and the dragon refusing to leave. Urdara broke a small branch from beside her and dropped it for the critter, which destroyed it immediately. Teiwa perked up.

"The branches," she said.

The others looked at her.

"You're gonna have to elaborate," Urdara replied.

"I can make us a bridge with the branches, and then we can escape. Wait."

She placed both hands on the trunk of the tree they sat on and concentrated. It was much harder for her to manipulate plants than it was to talk to them, but it was possible. She felt a little bad, but the trees could simply return to their normal position later. Slowly, the tree began to turn one direction towards another of its kind, which reached back to it. Their branches entwined, creating a bridge wide enough they could walk on, if they did so carefully. At'lokias raised his eyebrows and let out a whistle of admiration.

Step by step, they crossed from one tree to another, then another and so on as Teiwa created more and more bridges back towards the road. She often had to stop and ask for directions, but the trees were happy to answer her questions and soon they were close to a more recognizable area. The dragon, however, was still at their heels. She looked down and sighed as it growled up at her.

As they crossed from one tree to another and the dragon followed from the ground, the tree they climbed onto slapped at it with a wide branch. The dragon whined.

"Did you tell it to do that?" Urdara asked. Teiwa shook her head.

"I guess it's been watching us and it's tired of this whole thing," she replied, leaning down to watch.

The tree smacked it again. It tried to bite its branch, but got smacked a third time.

"Looks like we're going to be saved by a tree, which isn't even the weirdest way I've gotten out of trouble before." At'lokias shrugged.

Then it came. The louder noises caught up to them and from the shade emerged a much larger, but still not tall enough to reach them, t'rex dragon. It looked at its smaller friend and back up at the tree and roared. At'lokias gulped. Urdara clung to the tree.

"Do something," she whispered.

"Do what?" Teiwa whispered back.

The tree smacked the smaller dragon again and their eyes widened. The larger dragon stared up at it for a moment, seemingly considering its options. It hadn't been hit at all, so they had no way of knowing which side would win in a fight. Which would have been one very odd fight, too.

At last, it made a sound to the smaller dragon and started moving away. The smaller t'rex made a sound of disappointment in return and growled at the trio one last time before running off after its supposed parent.

They almost fell from the tree in their relief.

After that incident, travel was quiet again. They walked another day before reaching a town and stopping to rest. At'lokias left during the day to work odd jobs, and Urdara left at night for an entirely different reason. They gathered supplies and left again, this time on a merchant caravan. One morning, before they began moving again, At'lokias turned to them with a grin on his face.

"So, after our encounter with that tiny but very persistent dragon, I figured it wouldn't hurt to make sure we all can defend ourselves. I think we're far enough from town now that our practice won't cause any disturbances."

Urdara crossed her arms, already unimpressed by whatever he was about to suggest. Teiwa listened warily.

He opened his bag and pulled out a staff. Urdara snorted at how long it took him to pull the whole thing out. It was surreal and rather comical to watch how something so long could fit into such a normal sized bag. He tossed it to Teiwa and she caught it mid-air. The movement caught the attention of a couple caravaners, but they lost interest fairly quickly.

"That's your preferred weapon, isn't it? If that didn't change from when you used to sneak into the island guard practice grounds."

She rotated it back and forth in one hand for a bit, feeling the weight of it. "It hasn't changed, no."

He grinned as he pulled out a wooden sword from the bag.

"Did you just stick an entire armory in there or what?" Urdara raised an eyebrow.

"Shh, I'm trying to be cool," he protested. "All right, show me what you've got."

Teiwa stared at him for a moment, not sure she heard him right. When he decided she was taking too long, he lunged at her with his wooden sword. She yelped and flinched as she lifted the staff to defend herself.

"Come on, you can do better than that!" Urdara called out from the side, amused. She did not, in fact, know if she could.

At'lokias struck again and Teiwa nearly dropped her weapon as she tried to parry it. She attempted to catch it, but it danced mid-air as it constantly avoided her hands and she made a sound of frustration when at last it fell to the ground. At'lokias and Urdara snorted in sync.

"What happened? You used to be so good with that thing," At'lokias asked.

"Well, I haven't exactly practiced lately."

"When was the last time?" Urdara asked.

"Let's see, I was... Sixteen. Trex didn't like me handling weapons."

"I just dislike that guy more by the second." At'lokias grunted. Every time Trex was brought up, Teiwa seemed more and more meek. She'd given up just about everything about who she used to be since he'd abandoned the island, and while he was sure some of it had to do with being left with no friends, At'lokias couldn't help but wonder how much the boyfriend was to blame for it. It wouldn't surprise him if he were to find it was by his influence too that she started training under her father's guidance.

"Enough of that," Teiwa interrupted the subject. "Why don't we go over our travel plan? How far are we from Elwind now, again?"

At'lokias made a sound of displeasure as he placed the wooden sword back inside his bag. Rather than handing the staff back to him, Teiwa put it in hers. The gesture didn't go unnoticed by him and a smile tugged at the corner of his lips. If she was keeping it, then she planned on using it. Maybe that old Teiwa he knew wasn't entirely gone, after all.

Another few days of traveling went by uneventfully, for which the group was grateful. While it was rather boring to just walk or ride the wagon without anything else to do, it beat being chased by a dragon any day. Teiwa had been noticing a shape in the distance for a while, and the thought of the creature made her shiver. Could it be another, bigger one?

"Are we close yet?" Urdara asked as she crossed her arms behind her head and yawned.

At'lokias stopped walking and turned back towards them with a smile. He gestured towards something and the two women came closer to look.

Down the road, a large city sprawled ahead of them. Now that she saw the whole picture, she realized the shape she saw was a tall tower and was grateful that her suspicions were incorrect. Before it, there was a big lake with a strange shape by its coast.

At'lokias shot them a triumphant grin. "Ladies, I present to you El-wind."

II

ELWIND

"So this is where we part ways, it was a pleasure riding with you." At'lokias shook the hand of the lead caravaner and watched as he got back on his wagon.

The lake before them was vast and going around it would take time. That's what the caravaners would be doing now. Teiwa and Urdara watched the water expectantly.

"So how exactly do we cross?" Teiwa asked.

"Easy, we go by turtle," At'lokias replied.

The two stared at him.

"What? I'm serious. Look." He pointed towards odd, large shapes in the water and a man sitting by them. "Excuse me!"

The man stood and took hold of a rope that went into the water. He pulled on it and a head poked out. It was, indeed, a very large turtle. Its shell was flat and big enough to easily carry four or five people.

"You want to cross?" he asked. "One way trip is five silvies each. Round trip is eight."

At'lokias dug into his bag for money, but Urdara stopped him. "I got this," she said. "As long as you can guarantee that thing isn't going to throw me into the water."

Once she paid the man, he climbed onto the turtle's back and signaled for them to follow. He walked on it and sat by the head, where he pulled on the rope again. Reins.

"Won't we hurt it?" Teiwa asked.

"They do this all the time, it's fine. Come on," At'lokias called as he walked towards the animal. He stepped on it and reached out a hand to her.

She hesitated for a moment, so Urdara went ahead and climbed onto the shell. She looked to the man for instructions and he pointed down, so she found a spot that seemed reasonably safe and sat. Teiwa followed. Once both women were accommodated, At'lokias took a seat himself.

The man pulled on the reins and nudged the turtle's neck gently with a foot and it started moving. They sailed quietly across the lake. Halfway there, they passed another man on a turtle, bringing people in the opposite direction.

"See? Told you they do this all the time," At'lokias said.

Teiwa nodded. She pulled up her legs and rested her arms and head on her knees, smiling as she felt the breeze on her face. She looked to the side and found Urdara with her eyes closed, enjoying the weather as well. To her other side, At'lokias sat with a knee up and an arm resting on it. He looked at her and grinned.

***

The city of Elwind was unlike anything Teiwa had ever seen before. Rather than small houses, large buildings reached towards the sky, but none as tall as the tower right in the center of the city. The place had been built with a spiral layout and small side streets allowed one to move from one ring of the spiral to the next with ease.

At'lokias walked through the streets without trouble and Teiwa wondered how many times he'd been there before. Urdara, too, seemed oddly comfortable with the place. Above, movement caught her eye, but it was too fast for her to see exactly what it was. She shook her head and tried to focus on the path instead.

"Have you been here before?" Teiwa asked.

"A couple of times, though I never had to walk the whole way," she huffed. "It's a big city so there are good business opportunities here. Though I always came on my own carriage so I never had to ride a turtle before. Why, haven't you?"

"I haven't been anywhere." Teiwa shrugged.

"Oh, right."

At'lokias tried to hold back a laugh, but it came out a snort anyway. "That's not true anymore though, is it?"

Teiwa thought for a moment and nodded. He had a point. Even if she hadn't reached her destination yet, she'd gotten to see other places already and that had to count for something.

"All right, this way," he called out as he indicated a side street. They followed and on the other side, the inn waited for them, as imposing as every other building in the city. Its walls were white, much like most others, but flowers on every window gave it a more cheerful look. They seemed well tended to, which Teiwa appreciated.

At'lokias held the door open for them and they walked in to find the inside was just as clean looking as the outside. There were a few people hanging out by the tables, but it wasn't anywhere near as full as the inn where they'd been reunited days before. At'lokias greeted a few familiar faces before heading to the counter to arrange rooms for them.

Urdara leaned against a table and watched, bored. Teiwa followed, pulled back a chair and went to sit down.

"Loki!" a voice screamed from the front door and Teiwa nearly fell on the floor instead. Urdara jumped with surprise.

At'lokias turned around with a confused frown, but it disappeared the moment he saw who the voice belonged to. Instead, a bright smile took its place.

"Isarrel!" He rushed towards her, arms outstretched. She ran and jumped into his arms, a laugh escaping her lips as she did. He spun her around once before putting her back down.

Urdara and Teiwa just looked at each other. Urdara shrugged.

At'lokias guided the young woman over to the two, a smile still wide on his face. "Girls, this is Isarrel. She's a very dear friend of mine. Isarrel, these are Teiwa and Urdara."

Isarrel was a human, about the same height as Teiwa. Her blonde hair cascaded down her shoulders and to the middle of her back and her blue eyes sparkled as she greeted them. "I can't believe it, I've heard so much about you! You, especially," she said, her attention turned to Teiwa.

"But what are you doing here, anyway?" At'lokias asked quickly.

She turned back to face him. "Oh, I live here now! Or I will, after the wedding. Oh, you must come!"

He blinked. "Wedding? You're getting married? Do I know them?"

She shook her head. "You don't, but the two of you will get along great, I'm sure of it. You must come and meet her. Please? It's tonight, so I know this is a little close, but it would mean the world to me."

He looked to his friends as if looking for an answer to give her. She followed his eyes.

"Oh! And your friends are invited as well, of course! We would love to have you all."

"We didn't exactly pack clothes for the occasion," Urdara argued.

"No need! It's nothing too fancy, you can come wearing whatever you'd like. Please, it would mean so much."

At'lokias looked for a way out of it, but couldn't find any. In truth, he did want to go. Isarrel was a dear friend after all, and it's not every day that a close friend of yours gets married. He looked at the two of them. Urdara just shrugged.

"I suppose we can go," Teiwa added slowly.

Isarrel jumped in joy and threw herself at Teiwa, pulling her into a tight hug. "Thank you, thank you! I promise it'll be a lot of fun."

❧❧❧❧❧ ❧❧❧❧❧

As promised by Isarrel, the ceremony was simple. Though it had a great number of guests, no one's clothes were particularly ornate, not even the brides'. It took place at a public square, out in the open, and flowers and food were brought in by the family of Isarrel's bride, Makaea.

"With this, I declare you wedded. May your union last a lifetime and beyond," announced the priest as he pulled the veil over both their heads and the crowd exploded into cheers.

"I didn't expect there would be so many people," Teiwa said to At'lokias, almost screaming so she would be heard.

"I guess her bride's family is big, plus they're both very popular. Isarrel's family isn't too small, either."

"You guys have been friends long?" Urdara asked.

"Since we were twelve. We met when I went to Baysea to meet my grandmother, remember?" At'lokias replied.

"He saved Isarrel from a tree that was running out of control," a man put in from nearby, startling the trio.

At'lokias soon recognized the bride's brother and the two exchanged warm greetings. He turned to introduce him to the women, but was dragged away by him to greet the rest of the family. Teiwa and Urdara could do nothing but laugh.

⁂

"You won't guess what I found out." Urdara approached Teiwa with a wide grin.

It was the party after the wedding and the trio had been reunited and separated a number of times already. Urdara, apparently, used that opportunity to dig for information.

"What?" Teiwa asked in amusement. Someone passed by and handed her a drink. She took it with a timid thank you.

"Isarrel and Loki aren't just good friends. They used to be lovers." Urdara said in a singsong voice, waving her own drink around.

Teiwa spat the drink she'd just taken a sip of.

"So according to... I don't know who this is according to anymore, I talked to so many people." Urdara looked around with a frown. "That guy there, maybe. According to him or maybe someone else, after Loki left the island he spent a good while living in Baysea, which is where Isarrel also lived, and the two got closer, and then some more. And now we're all at her wedding, isn't that weird?"

Teiwa frowned. "What's weird is you spent the party digging for that information." She looked ahead and saw a man coming towards them. "Oh, I hope it's not someone asking me to dance again." She felt like she'd danced with just about every man in that party, and a good part of the women as well.

Urdara raised an eyebrow. "You can just say no, you know."

Teiwa made a sound of discomfort. "I don't feel like I can."

The man approached them and spread his arms wide. "My lady! Would you care for a dance?"

"She's not interested," Urdara replied for her.

He frowned. "I believe I was talking to the other lady."

"Look, she's not interested and if you don't leave it be, I'll make sure you regret that choice." She crossed her arms in front of her chest, somehow not spilling her drink in the process. She looked him up and down and harrumphed.

The man looked frustrated, but also a little frightened as he left.

"What were you going to do if he didn't leave?" Teiwa asked.

Urdara shrugged. "Doesn't matter. All that matters is convincing him it's gonna be bad. It's all about the appearances. I'm not even strong." She laughed.

Teiwa laughed as well. "Why, thank you then."

As the two drank, Isarrel approached from the crowd. "May I sit with you two for a moment?" she asked, smiling.

Urdara made a gesture to indicate yes and she took a seat next to Teiwa.

"I hope you're enjoying the party. We wanted to make sure it would be fun, above all else."

"Oh, it's been great fun," Urdara replied with a grin. Teiwa resisted the urge to groan.

"I understand you've been asking around about me," the bride asked, her eyes narrowing with her smile.

Urdara was unfazed. "If it helps, I was mostly asking about Loki. I don't know you, and I don't care to."

Isarrel sat back on her chair with a content sigh. "That's fine with me. I do love him, you know."

Teiwa spit her drink for the second time. She had to start picking better moments to take sips. She looked down at her clothes to make sure she hadn't stained them.

"Not like that," Isarrel laughed. "But I'll always love him in a way. He was a precious part of my life, even if he broke my heart back then."

Teiwa frowned. She couldn't imagine referring to Trex in that same manner. The time they'd spent together had been wonderful, but it was marred by the way he ended it all.

It was their anniversary and he'd asked to speak to her in their favorite place, a quiet clearing by the lake. She'd thought he'd ask her to marry him, but instead he informed her he had no intention to continue their relationship. That he didn't love her, and never had. How was she to consider him precious to her after such a thing? Though she supposed Loki would never do something like that. Surely Isarrel's heartbreak had been much, much kinder.

"How come?" Urdara asked, bringing Teiwa back from her thoughts.

"We'd never intended for it to mean anything," Isarrel started. "We were just kids, experimenting, you know? We were what, fifteen? I caught feelings, he didn't. I knew from the start he would never be mine, not really. His heart already belonged to someone else. And what little hope started to blossom, he crushed. Gently, of course. He's always gentle about it." She sighed.

"He was already in love with someone else?" Urdara's grin widened.

Teiwa hadn't paid special attention to that information, but now it intrigued her. If he was fifteen, that was shortly after he left the island. Could it be someone from there? Or had he met someone at Baysea, so quickly after moving in?

"He still is, I think. But it's fine. I have Makaea now, and I've come to love him as someone important to me, without the romance. Whether he likes it or not, he's part of why I am who I am today, and I think that's precious. Don't you?" She smiled again, raised her glass at them as she stood, and left.

Elsewhere, At'lokias had just walked away from a conversation with some of Isarrel's family members. He turned to look for Teiwa and Urdara when a woman approached him. She was exceedingly average looking, the kind of person whose face he knew he would forget the moment she left. And though he'd never seen her before, he knew exactly who it was.

"Oh, now you show up," he said and crossed his arms in frustration. "I've been trying to talk to you for days."

"I am here now. Speak."

"We're in the middle of the party."

"You should be used to this by now."

He looked around and sighed. "Fine. What's with all this? We had a deal. I thought I had more time."

"And yet you didn't," the woman said. "But this was not my doing."

"Are you saying you had nothing to do with whatever got Teiwa to start this journey to Yrathea?"

"I have no control over forbidden magic, you know that. I didn't even get to witness what happened to that poor man, though I heard it was quite.... unfortunate. I, too, believed we had more time."

He watched her for a moment, unsure. "And that message, was it really from Yrathea?"

"Why would it not be?"

"I don't know. Was it?"

"I do not speak the sylvan tongue, so I did not hear the message, but I watched as she did. I have no reason to believe it came from anyone else.

My connection to Yrathea is more of an empathic one, and I know her to be growing weary from the foreign magic in her roots."

He looked around, avoiding her gaze for a moment. "All right, I believe you."

"Of course you do, my people do not lie."

"You know what I mean." He sighed. "So anyway, how about—" He turned to look at her again, but she was gone. "Of course."

He walked over to his friends and offered Teiwa a dance. This time, when she said yes, she meant it.

12
THE LIBRARY

The Great Library of Elwind was located in the tallest tower in the city, right in the center. Teiwa looked up at it as they approached and felt dizzy from how tall it was. She'd never seen a building of that size before. Somewhere from the top, figures flew in and out of the tower, but against the sun it was hard to make out their shapes.

"Oh, those are dragons," At'lokias said, noticing where she was looking. "The city uses them to send messages and letters, both within the city limits and out. It's why we didn't see a guinatee at the inn. They have one in the town hall, though. Kind of the opposite of Eastlake where there's a dragon in the town hall and guinatees at most places."

"You know a lot about this city," Urdara put in from the other side.

"I've been here plenty of times, it's a popular destination for my clients." At'lokias shrugged. "Now, before we go in, we should figure out what type of books exactly we're after. They're not big on conversations inside."

Teiwa crossed her arms and thought for a moment. There would certainly not be any books on how to save Yrathea. If anyone knew that, surely they'd have done it rather than write a book about it. "Magic books, perhaps?"

"How about books on forbidden magic? It's been around for a good while, according to the stories. Even if not everyone believes it's real, surely there have been people who studied it, right?" Urdara suggested.

Teiwa nodded. "Yes, that sounds good."

"All right, books on forbidden magic then." At'lokias agreed. He moved to the door and held it open for them. "Ladies first, love." He winked at Teiwa.

"Love?" she asked, a hint of amusement in her voice.

"Just a term of endearment, that's all."

"Ah," was all she said before going inside. Urdara went after her, a strong feeling of judgment in her gaze. He followed them inside and closed the door behind him.

The library looked even bigger from the inside, though Teiwa knew that wasn't possible. Then again, neither was Loki's bag. She wondered if there was some sort of magic at play in that place, or if it was just an impression. A stairway followed a spiral pattern inside the tower, leading to numerous floors full of shelves filled to the brim with books. People circulated freely between them, but just as At'lokias had warned them, everything was awfully quiet. It was almost disconcerting.

"Now," he whispered, "you two wait here and I'll find us a librarian."

The two nodded at him and At'lokias left. He located a woman not far from the entrance, arranging a pile of books. He approached her as quietly as he could.

"Excuse me," he whispered. No reply. "Excuse me." Still nothing. She apparently hadn't heard him, so he decided to raise his voice a little bit. "Excuse me."

She turned around angrily and shushed him.

"I'm sorry—I was just—I'm just—I'm trying—to ask—you—a question," he said, interrupted by her shushing every few words. He stared at her.

"Questions are for those who can speak at a reasonable level," she replied, only slightly lower than him.

"I'm sorry," he tried speaking again, careful to level his voice with hers, "I was just wondering if you have any books on forbidden magic."

She looked up and down at him, eyes narrowed. "We do," she said, "but not for you. Only those with special permissions may read those books."

He pursed his lips. How she even knew he didn't have special permission was beyond him, but he decided not to dwell on that. He thanked her and walked back to his friends.

"Good news and bad news. Good news is they have books on forbidden magic. Bad news is we're not allowed near them."

"What?" Urdara exclaimed and a wave of shushing traveled down the entire library. She flinched. Teiwa didn't say anything, but flinched along with her.

"What?" Teiwa repeated, lower. "So what do we do?"

He shrugged. "We find a way to get special permission, I guess." At'lokias said and turned back toward the exit when a voice interrupted him.

"At'lokias," someone called from further into the library, their voice just loud enough to hear but not enough to be a problem.

The trio turned around to find a woman, young looking, unlike any other in the library. Her skin was white as porcelain, to the point Teiwa wondered if blood ran through her veins at all. It was paler than any skin she'd ever seen. Her hair was white and long, tied in dozens of tiny braids adorned with golden rings. Her features were thin and delicate, her neck oddly long and her eyes a strange mix between purple, pink and blue. Even her pupils were so light, they were barely visible against her irises. She wore a twisted golden top and a long, open skirt with gold detailing. Goldweaving spider silk, Teiwa noted. But in that amount, she couldn't imagine the cost. The woman practically floated towards them, her movements so fluid it was like the air itself bent to her will. She smiled. "I thought that was you."

At'lokias stared at her in surprise. "Aira? What are you doing here? No, nevermind, that's a stupid question. How did you know I was here?"

"Your loud friend caught my attention and in turning to look, I noticed you in her company. Long time no see, I trust you have been well."

Urdara wanted to complain, but even she didn't have the courage to argue against a light elf. At'lokias turned to her and Teiwa.

"This is Aira. She's a friend of mine."

"Is there anyone out there who isn't a friend of yours?" Urdara questioned.

"Probably."

"It is a pleasure to make your acquaintance," the woman said, "I am Ethairadel, but you may refer to me as Aira, should that suit you better."

How in the world was Loki friends with a light elf? They all lived in the Sacred City and only a few select ones ever left, and even those only did so to assist in important matters. That he'd met and befriended one was beyond belief. Then again, Teiwa thought, he did say he got his magic bags from them. Was he friends with more than one? Or had Aira been the one to supply them?

"These are Teiwa and Urdara," At'lokias motioned to them as he spoke.

Ethairadel raised one hand with her palm up and another in the opposite manner, forming a circle between them, and held them out in front of her chest as she bowed, turned slightly more towards Teiwa. She appreciated the greeting common to her mother's people and offered the same in return. To Urdara, Ethairadel just bowed and received a similar gesture in return.

"You know," At'lokias started, careful to keep his voice level, "running into you here might be exactly what we need."

Ethairadel observed him for a moment before she spoke again. "You require special permission to access certain books."

The trio blinked in surprise. "How did you—" Urdara started.

"We are in the Great Library of Elwind. At'lokias was turning to leave when I approached. My presence is convenient. He must require special permission."

It was almost infuriating. Urdara wondered how anyone could be friends with someone like that. Yet, she couldn't argue the advantages of it. "So, can you help?" she asked.

Ethairadel nodded slightly and, without waiting for them, sought a librarian. She returned moments later. "You may read what ever books you desire, so long as I accompany you. Come, show me what you need."

Several floors above ground, the group looked through shelves upon shelves of books on magic and forbidden magic both. At'lokias glossed over a few titles when a voice came from just above his shoulder.

"Take that one."

He jumped and turned to look. There was no one. He rolled his eyes.

"What, are you haunting me now?" he whispered.

A woman, completely different from the one at the wedding and yet as remarkably bland as her, appeared in front of him. She blinked.

"Haunting is a thing ghosts do. I am not a ghost," she said.

"It's just a manner of speech. All right, what other books do you want me to take?"

She shrugged. "It does not matter, Ethairadel has already taken the ones that do. I only suggested that because it looked interesting."

He resisted the urge to roll his eyes again. "Very well, thank you for the suggestion. Now, if you'll excuse me, I'm a little busy right now."

She chuckled. "You amuse me. Go ahead, then."

He took the book along with a few others and carried them back to the desk where Ethairadel already waited with a pile of her own. Urdara and Teiwa soon joined the two and the group set to reading.

"Check this out, this book tells of a man who grew a second pair of hands, right above the original ones. Gross," Urdara said.

Teiwa made a face. "That's horrible."

"This one tells of a woman who gave birth to some weird blob of goo." At'lokias added.

"I don't think this is what we're looking for," Teiwa said.

"It's not my fault all these books are about the horrors of foreign magic, but none about how to stop it."

"This one tells the story of how it came into our world and the history of the city it first entered through. Although I was already aware of it, perhaps it interests one of you?" Ethairadel nudged a book towards them.

"Everyone knows the story already," Urdara argued. "It doesn't help us stop it."

Teiwa pulled it to herself. "I want to read it. Maybe there's something in the history of Everfall that can be of use."

"Suit yourself." Urdara shrugged and went back to reading disgusting stories in her own book.

At'lokias looked to Ethairadel and she shot him a brief but knowing look. He looked back down at his book without saying anything.

Hours passed and At'lokias and Urdara had both finished their initial books and taken on other ones from their piles when Teiwa looked up from hers.

"I think I've found something," she said.

They all turned to look at her with interest.

"Everfall was the sister city of the Sacred City, was it not, Ethairadel?" she asked.

"That is correct," Ethairadel said.

"It says here that the light elves trusted the people of Everfall with a number of magical artifacts for safekeeping. It especially mentions an orb capable of absorbing magic. If it can absorb our magic, perhaps it's capable of absorbing forbidden magic as well?"

Ethairadel leaned over to glance at the book without demonstrating much interest. "Yes, that is possible. However, that is one of the artifacts we did not recover before the fall of Everfall."

Urdara snorted. At'lokias and Teiwa glowered at her and she smirked back at them. Ethairadel seemed unaffected.

"That is a viable theory," she continued, "but I am afraid in order to test it, you must first recover the orb from the ruins of Everfall. I cannot assist you in this task, my people cannot enter that city."

"Because of the forbidden magic?" At'lokias asked.

"That is one of the reasons. Forbidden magic is fatal to our kind. Even a light exposure to it is enough to kill. But we are also incapable of going past the magic seals placed at every gate. When the people of Everfall brought forbidden magic into our world, they set those seals so those of higher connection to Yrathea would not be able to pass. That includes my people and the gods themselves."

"The gods can't enter?" Teiwa's eyes widened. "How is that possible?"

"The gods' power is tied directly to Yrathea and her magic. Because forbidden magic is not of this world, they have no power over it. It can, oftentimes, even weaken their original abilities greatly. Should you choose to go, you will be on your own."

Teiwa fell back in her chair.

"That's not true," At'lokias put in, "she'll have us."

"For all the good that does." Urdara rolled her eyes.

"So, Teiwa, what is it that you wish to do?" Ethairadel asked.

"I suppose... We're going to Everfall."

13

SILK

A few days prior, Ethairadel had been at the Sacred City.

"And that concludes our lesson," said the teacher as she closed the book in her hand. "I will now read your assignments. You may leave once you have heard yours."

Ethairadel sat among numerous other young light elves. Still short of two hundred years old, she still had several hundred years worth of lessons to learn. She would only be considered a proper adult at five hundred years of age.

"Ethairadel," called the teacher, "you are to collect silk today."

Ethairadel stood up, bowed to her teacher, and left the room. As far as assignments went, this was a welcome one. She rather enjoyed spending time with the goldweaving spiders. Fascinating creatures, really, and a big asset to their city. They coexisted peacefully, without keeping them in enclosures, and they often chose a few specific areas to live in and make their webs.

She walked down the stairs and across the plaza when she felt observed and turned around. There was a dragon, much larger than her, but still small compared to the others that lived in the city, stalking after her. She smiled.

"What do you think you are doing?" It wiggled its behind at her in a playful gesture and she chuckled. "I do not have time to play, I am on silk duty."

It seemed to deflate. From behind it, a much smaller dragon, roughly the size of a large house cat, ran towards Ethairadel and between her legs. She put her hands on her hips and inclined her head in a mock gesture of exasperation.

"And you have brought your brother with you, as well." She picked up the smaller dragon and gave its head a little kiss. "But I am afraid that changes nothing, I must get to the spiders. I will play with you when I am finished." She put the dragon back down, patted the larger one on its head, and left.

The spiders' nest was unlike any other to be found outside of the Sacred City. Its gold strands sparkled in the sun and created beautiful patterns as the spiders weaved their webs. Ethairadel approached carefully and examined the scene, looking for extra silk she could remove without disturbing them. It was very common for them to produce far more than they needed, as they did not stop weaving strands after creating their homes. Nearby, a long tool sat idly by. She picked it up, placed it in a web that was unused and began to twist. Upon collecting the first one, she moved on to the next. By the time she was done with that nest, she had a reasonable amount of silk ready to process. She placed it in a basket and moved on to the next nest.

The sun was beginning to set when she left the silk to be processed. She did not have any further assignments for the day, so she sought out the young dragons, but they were nowhere to be seen. Probably shooed away by one of the more impatient elders.

She walked down a few streets, up a few sets of stairs and stopped by a window to observe the city. It was her home and all she'd ever known for the better part of her life, but she still found it beautiful. The city rose in large and imposing spiraling towers of marble white, though most were covered in either plants, gold spider silk, or both. The rooftops pointed up at the sky in golden spirals, their shingles made with silk mixed in as well. It was one of the most common materials in the city, but still highly valued and used in as many areas as they could. It sparkled beautifully in the sun and gave the entire city an ethereal feeling. And south, by the edge of the city, stood Yrathea, the World Tree, Life of All.

It towered over the buildings. Its branches reached far and created shade for a good portion of the city under it, and by its base several smaller trees grew out of its roots. Its trunk was thick enough one could build inside it, if they so desired, and covered with smaller plants and moss. Truly, it was a magnificent sight, and one Ethairadel was grateful for every day.

She continued up the stairs and towards a doorway that led to one of the many branches of the library. Because of its enormous size, it was divided in multiple areas throughout the city. It was considered one single library, despite its numerous locations, as they were all connected and separated by subject.

Ethairadel entered and was greeted silently by the librarian at the entrance. She returned the quiet greeting and moved to the shelves she was after without missing a beat or needing to check. She'd grown up in the many library branches in the city and this was one of the most familiar to her.

The book she sought was far down the corridors and it took her time to reach it, but she did so with practiced ease. As she picked it up and opened it, a voice whispered in her ear.

"Hello."

She jumped and turned around, though she already knew who it belonged to. There was only one person who would dare sneak up on her like that. Not because she was particularly dangerous, but because light elves had no sense of humor.

The woman before her was stunning. Her skin was the same pale white as Ethairadel, but her hair was a blue so dark it neared black, with small crystals spread all over it to mimic stars. Her features were sharp and perfectly balanced and her gown and hair seemed to flow around her as if she were underwater. Her eyes were pure white, no iris or pupil to be seen. She smiled a genuine looking smile.

"I have not seen you in a good while," Ethairadel said with a smile. "That is a beautiful form you have taken."

"Do you like it? Is the flowing too much? I like looking the part when I can." She grinned, hair and gown flowing about behind her.

"No, it is the perfect godly look for you. Is this a personal visit? We have not had one in a few months now." Ethairadel asked.

"I'm afraid not. I do want to have a personal visit soon, but right now, I have a task for you."

"A task? Very well, I am always ready to serve. What is it you need of me?"

"I need you to meet up with At'lokias in Elwind."

14

WARNINGS

"Before you depart, there are things you must be made aware of," Ethairadel said, opening the book she'd borrowed from the library. Normally they would not allow it to leave the building, but as a light elf she had special permission to do just about whatever she desired.

Teiwa, At'lokias and Urdara were sitting on a bed in their room in the inn, where they were sure they would not be interrupted or heard. The three nodded along almost in sync.

"First of all, the orb is very powerful and we do not have a full grasp on everything it can do. When it was entrusted to the people of Everfall, it was a powerful magic absorbent, but after we lost contact with them, it is possible they may have experimented with or modified it. It is also possible they have set it as a trap. You are to treat it with extreme caution. Under no circumstances should you touch the orb barehanded."

"So we wrap it before we take it, that's easy enough," said Urdara with a shrug. "What else?"

"It is also possible the building it is in has traps set up inside. We have not been able to enter the city for a long time, so I cannot give you more accurate warnings. Be careful where you step and what you touch."

"So don't touch the orb, don't touch the walls, don't touch just about anything, right?" At'lokias crossed his arms.

"Unless you must, yes."

"That's gonna be a fun time." He rolled his eyes.

Ethairadel blinked. "It is not likely to be fun. Your goal is to retrieve the orb, not entertain yourselves."

"No, I meant... Nevermind." He sighed.

"There is another thing I must warn you about," she continued. "As you may remember, due to the forbidden magic and the seals around the city, not only my kind has been unable to enter Everfall since before its fall..."

Urdara snickered. At'lokias elbowed her on the ribs.

Ethairadel remained unaffected. "The gods, too, have not been able to enter for a long time. While this break in the connection to the gods and Yrathea are what led to its demise, the majority of the people of Everfall did not leave until it was too late. There are thousands of dead in that city, and Death has not been able to claim them."

"I'm sorry, what?" At'lokias blinked.

"Death cannot enter places infested with forbidden magic. He cannot even see into them. The souls of all the dead in Everfall are still there. It has been centuries, so experience tells us they have all turned into wraiths by now."

"So wraiths aren't just a story either? Gods!" At'lokias exclaimed.

"The stories may exaggerate a little, but they are mostly true. Souls left in this world after their death do become twisted with time and turn into horrible creatures. You will likely see them there. There is no telling whether they will be aggressive towards you. Some wraiths are, but there have been cases where they simply wander, lost in their thoughts, if they still have any. It is possible you will be lucky. But with how many there will be, I would not count on luck alone."

"Then what would you count on?" Urdara asked.

"You are to avoid them whenever possible. They are not likely to see you from a distance or if you hide behind something. They are not known to be great hunters. If you find yourself face to face with them, I believe running is the best route." She closed the book in her hand. Then, almost as an afterthought, she added to it. "And surely I do not need to tell you not to let them take the orb from you."

"Are we to expect them to try and take the orb?" Teiwa asked.

Ethairadel shrugged, the gesture seeming foreign considering her usual demeanor. "I do not know, I am not a wraith."

⁂

Teiwa played the scene in her mind over and over again during the trip, trying to remember Ethairadel's advice. They rented a wagon from a merchant caravan that was leaving Elwind to the city closest to the ruins, which made travel much easier. Urdara complained about the lack of comfort, and Teiwa had to agree with her, but not out loud. Never out loud, lest she let it get to her head. At'lokias, on the other hand, was used to much worse.

Though the going was slow, it was not worse than the time they'd have made by foot, and the wagon meant they had a space to rest whenever they wanted. At'lokias walked through most of the day, too restless to stay inside with the two young women. Urdara was the complete opposite, though she felt restless, she did not seek to exert herself anymore than she absolutely needed to. Teiwa tried to be a bit of both so neither side felt abandoned. She walked with At'lokias for part of the day, and sat with Urdara when she felt tired.

They'd been traveling for a few days when it happened.

At'lokias woke up in an unfamiliar location. His head was resting against someone's lap and he glanced up to find his mother stroking his hair gently. He sat up. The entire room seemed oddly blue.

"Mom?"

She smiled sweetly at him. "Hello, dear."

He cocked his head to the side, but couldn't find the words to ask any of the questions swirling around in his head.

"Look at you," she said, "all grown up. You've gotten so handsome, just like your father."

He looked very little like his father, he thought, but that was still the least of his concerns. He opened his mouth to speak, but no words came out. In fact, he wasn't sure what he'd wanted to say in the first place. Everything was confusing and he felt dizzy and tired. She stroked his cheek.

"Why don't you lie down some more? I can tell you need it. Come, love, I'll stroke your hair until you fall asleep."

He obeyed slowly. The moment his head was on her lap again, he felt incredibly heavy. His eyelids fought him and he couldn't stand to keep them open a moment longer. His mother hummed a song as he drifted off.

A drop of water hit his face, and another. He struggled to open his eyes.

His mother was staring down at him through empty eye sockets, water running down them like an overflowing bucket as it spilled. She still smiled.

He woke with a start. Tears mixing with cold sweat, he hugged his knees and took a long, deep breath. He looked around. He couldn't tell if he'd screamed, but if he did, he didn't wake Urdara. Teiwa, however, was nowhere to be found. At'lokias rubbed his face with a hand and moved to the back of the wagon.

Outside, Teiwa stood alone among the caravan's various wagons. Everyone slept soundly and she held the staff he'd given her the other day in her hands. She stood in position and struck against the air, again and again. Then she changed stances and practiced her attack from another angle.

He leaned against the wall and sighed, content. Maybe the night wasn't that terrible, after all.

15

FALSE STARTS

"What do you think it's like?" a thirteen year old Teiwa asked.

"What do I think what's like?" fifteen year old At'lokias asked in response.

"Liking someone."

He froze in place. She said it so casually and, luckily for him, didn't seem to notice his reaction. The last thing he wanted was to be questioned about that.

"I don't know," he lied.

"I asked A'mma about it. She thought it was cute." She crossed her arms and pouted.

He thought she was cute, too, but he wasn't about to say that. When he didn't answer, she continued.

"She said it's like home. Like Papa is her home. So it doesn't matter where she is, she knows she can always go back to him."

"That sounds nice," he said.

"It also sounds wrong." She frowned. "Everyone talks about the butterflies or whatever. She said I'll understand it someday, but I wanna know now."

"Well, you can't make yourself like someone just because you're curious... I think."

"Don't you wanna know?"

Except he already did. He frowned. Surely this whole thing was Urdara's fault. First Teiwa had started to grow her hair—now a little below her chin—because she wanted to be pretty like their friend, and now this. He missed being younger and not having to deal with these complicated feelings.

"You know what else I'm curious about? Kissing."

His eyes widened more than he thought they could as he looked at her.

"Everyone makes such a big deal about it, aren't you curious?"

"Uh, I don't know. I guess?"

He wanted to slap himself. Why would he give her reason to go on with that conversation? He should have shut it down the moment it started.

"Come on, let's try it!" She almost jumped as she turned to face him better.

He swallowed. This was not how he thought their day was going to go. Alarm bells rang on his head, but he couldn't think of a single way to escape it. Did he want to escape it? Yes, he decided. Definitely yes.

"I don't know if we should—" he started.

"Come on, it'll be quick! Just to see what it's like." She grinned at him and he thought he just might pass out from the whole thing.

"A-all right... I guess..."

"Close your eyes then," she ordered.

He did as he was told. His heart rang in his ears and he could swear he was sweating. She closed her eyes and pressed her lips a little too hard against his. He shut his eyes tighter and the two stayed that way for a moment before she pulled back. When he opened his eyes, she looked frustrated.

"Maybe we're doing it wrong," he suggested and immediately regretted it.

She considered this for a moment. "But what else is there to do? That's how you kiss, right? Just press your lips together?"

He shrugged. He had just as much experience with this as she did.

"This sucks. I didn't feel any butterflies."

He definitely did.

❧ ❧

When At'lokias woke up, Urdara was watching him with a grin and he almost jumped.

"What?"

"Oh, nothing," she said in a voice that made it clear there was definitely something. "You just must be glad Tei is still asleep." Her grin widened.

He felt his blood run cold. "What are you talking about?"

"You were calling out to her in your sleep. 'Oh, Tei, kiss me,'" she said in a mocking voice.

He stared at her for a time. "No, I wasn't."

"No, you weren't." She shrugged. "But you should have seen your face for a moment."

He could have slapped her. He would never know, but though she did exaggerate it, he was indeed calling out for Teiwa in his sleep.

Not too long after that, the leader of the caravan knocked on their wagon to inform them it was time to move. Teiwa woke up from the knocking and failed to understand what Urdara thought was so funny, but neither side was willing to offer her an explanation.

That afternoon, the group arrived at their destination, the city of Stonebrook. The caravan would continue their journey without them from here on out. They found an inn and spent the night.

The three set out first thing in the morning towards the ruins of Everfall. From the map, they estimated they must be about a day and a half away, but they still had more than enough supplies.

They walked at an easy pace, with Teiwa admiring the trees and plants as they went and pausing now and then to collect samples of herbs she happened to see.

"So, how do you think that orb works?" Urdara asked.

"It absorbs magic, right? Maybe you just... Leave it next to what you want it to absorb?" Teiwa said, looking up in thought.

"That sounds dangerous, there must be a way to keep it from absorbing magic from everything. Or everyone," At'lokias added.

Teiwa thought for another moment and nodded in agreement.

"That doesn't really answer my question, then," Urdara argued.

"Aira said she would do more research, maybe by the time she meets us in Stonebrook she'll have information on how to use it. And besides, after this we're headed to the Sacred City, right? Someone there is bound to know that," At'lokias replied.

Urdara just made a sound of agreement and left it at that. It was all she could do to hope he was right.

Not long after, the trees around them started to shift from their usual green to a blackened, dead appearance. Teiwa shivered and stopped to put on her shoes, not wanting to facilitate a connection with them, if it was at all still possible.

By sundown, the trio reached a large wall in ruins.

"I thought this place was supposed to be farther away," Urdara said, suspicious.

"I thought so, too." At'lokias stretched to try to see over it.

A little farther down, Teiwa found the entrance and waved at them to come over.

"Looks like it's a city," she said, "so I guess we're here."

The three entered cautiously. The place was in ruins, but its state was even worse than they'd expected. Some buildings had fallen apart and others looked precariously close to it. Moss grew on just about every surface and a strange, black goo was present in a number of places. Urdara considered touching it to see what it was, but decided against it.

"So the orb is supposed to be within a tower, right?" Teiwa asked as she turned in circles to look around herself. "I don't see any."

"Maybe it's collapsed." At'lokias joined her in her circling.

"You mean to tell me we'll have to dig it out of wherever the tower was? How do we even know it's not smashed to pieces?" Urdara protested. "Stop circling around, you two look ridiculous."

Teiwa made a sound of annoyance, but did as she was told. At'lokias continued for another moment, a grin on his face whenever he turned to face Urdara, who rolled her eyes at him.

"Well, if the tower was important, it's probably in the center of the city, right?" Teiwa ventured. "So if we find the center, we ought to find the tower, or what's left of it. If this is the entrance, and this looks like a main street, we should be able to find a main square if we just continue in this direction." She pointed.

They didn't have to walk long to find the main square. At'lokias looked around and scratched his head.

"There's something wrong," he said. "This place is too small."

"You're right, we found the square way too quickly. And there's no sign of there having been a tower around here, either." Urdara agreed, though she hated to do so.

At'lokias found a rock that didn't seem covered in moss and sat on it. When he took the map out of his bag and opened it, Teiwa approached and sat on his lap to look. He stiffened.

"What are you doing?" he asked.

"Looking at the map," she replied, not turning to face him.

He looked at Urdara with an expression of panic, but she just snorted a laugh. Teiwa was completely unaware of his discomfort and continued her examination.

"I think this isn't the right place," she said, "but whatever this place is, it's not on the map. Maybe it's this mark over here?" She pointed at a small symbol.

Urdara approached them from behind and leaned forward to look at the map as well. "That just means we have to keep walking. If we continue down this street, maybe we'll come out on the other side of this city and then we can continue towards the ruins. The right ones, this time. It's odd that this place isn't marked properly, though. Maybe it's superstition, I've heard before that some maps don't carry markings of places they consider... Evil? Not that this place looks anything more than just run down. Besides, if that's the case you'd think they wouldn't mark Everfall either. So who's to say that's the reasoning behind it."

Teiwa nodded in agreement and stood up, allowing At'lokias to release the breath he'd been holding. He folded the map again and placed it back inside his bag.

The three turned to continue their walk, when something caught their attention at the edge of their sight.

"What is that?" Teiwa asked. "It looks like it's moving."

The figure continued to approach them slowly. At'lokias' eyes widened and he pushed the two into a hole in one of the buildings, pressing hard against them.

Squeezed between Urdara and At'lokias, Teiwa couldn't see what it was. She turned her face to At'lokias to ask, but was stricken by the sudden realization of just how tall he was. She'd noticed he'd grown taller than her, and had found it rather frustrating, but she hadn't realized by just how much. No, he wasn't just tall now, but wider too. She hadn't paid attention before to just how large he'd gotten. Pressed hard against him like that, it was impossible not to notice. Her thoughts flashed back to the seamstresses and his shirtless torso and heat crawled up her chest and into her face and ears. She shook her head as if to scare the thought away.

Behind her, Urdara gasped dramatically for air. "What is it?" she asked in a loud whisper.

At'lokias shushed her and turned his head to look.

"What... Is it?" she asked again, slightly lower but angrier this time.

"I think... It's a wraith."

16
WRAITH

The creature wandered down the street, seemingly without purpose. In the corner where they hid, Urdara's eyes widened.

"I thought those were stuck in Everfall," she whispered.

"Clearly this one didn't get the memo," At'lokias replied, still facing away from them to watch the wraith.

"So what do we do?" Urdara asked.

"I suggest we stay quiet, for one," he whispered angrily at her.

Urdara frowned, but he wasn't looking her way. Even if he were, she suspected he wouldn't care about it. Teiwa shot her an apologetic look that made no difference whatsoever.

The creature turned in their direction and At'lokias pushed them deeper into the ruin. When it continued walking towards them, he unsheathed the sword at his side and waited.

The wraith stopped moving and watched for a while, as if it were trying to determine what it was seeing. How well could it see? Just as At'lokias wondered about that, it let out a shriek and started moving faster towards the group. He cursed.

"You two stay right here," he ordered.

He stepped out of the ruins cautiously, sword in hand. The creature stopped its movement again and watched him. At'lokias moved farther to the side, trying to guide the wraith towards the square. It worked. The monster followed, its movements jerky and uneven. It didn't seem to notice the two young women still left in the ruins of the building.

At'lokias and the monster stared at each other for a time, then the creature lunged. At'lokias ducked and raised his sword, but it went right through its body without causing any damage. He spit out an oath.

The wraith turned around and went for him again. It was a little taller than him, its skin an odd shade of purple, hanging from its apparent bones like one might hang clothes out to dry. It looked terribly hungry.

It went for another attack, deformed hands with strong claws out in front of it and At'lokias parried with his sword. He tried to slash at its arm and the sword went right through again.

"How does that thing even work?" he exclaimed, mostly to himself.

It slashed again and its claws connected with his arm, tearing a scream from his throat. Teiwa tried to run out of the ruins to meet him but was stopped by Urdara, who shook her head at her.

"He said to stay here. You'll just get in the way," she whispered.

Teiwa looked in their direction and sighed. Urdara was right, she had no experience fighting and would probably only serve to give At'lokias something else to worry about. Still, it was her friend out there fighting that thing, and she wished more than anything that she could be useful to him.

At'lokias continued to slash at the creature, trying to find a part with a physical form he could cut through, but only its claws, and presumably its teeth, seemed to really be there. The rest was almost an illusion, a memory of what it once used to be. The monster lunged at him again and he parried, but he knew he couldn't keep this up forever. No matter how many openings he took, if he couldn't kill his adversary, it would inevitably kill him instead. And then what would become of Teiwa and Urdara?

Would it find them? Would they starve to death in that corner, hiding from it until their demise?

The wraith slammed at him with its arm, surprisingly physical, and it threw him off his balance. At'lokias fell on the ground and hurried to regain his footing before the creature came at him again, but it was too late. It was already upon him and it came down on him hard with that arm. It was all At'lokias could do to raise his sword and try to lessen the impact, but the moment the arm connected, the earth gave out under him and he fell into a hole with a curse.

Teiwa held back a scream as she saw him disappear into the ground. She covered her mouth with both her hands and Urdara looked at her with an unsaid question, but she didn't know how to explain exactly what had happened.

At'lokias spat another oath as he rubbed his back and looked around for his sword. The creature was still up on the ground level, and there didn't seem to be any others down there with him. A small blessing he was grateful for. He looked up at the wraith. It watched him, seemingly weighing its options. Maybe it didn't know how to climb back out and was afraid of jumping in. It certainly didn't look like that fall had been part of its plan, if it had any. He wasn't sure just how intelligent the monster was, but one thing was clear. Whatever trace of humanity it'd had, it had disappeared along with its physical form.

"Wraiths are mostly magic left over," he whispered to himself. So maybe magic could affect it. It was worth a shot, if nothing else.

Rather than picking up his sword, he focused on the creature above him and made a lifting motion with his hands. Fire licked up the wraith from the feet up and it let out an ear-splitting scream. The women covered their ears, but At'lokias resisted the urge in order to summon more fire. Slowly, it consumed the body of the monster until there was nothing left.

Teiwa released a breath and ran towards the hole. Urdara protested but chased after her.

"Are you all right down there?" Teiwa called out to her friend.

"I'm fine," he replied. "I think this is a tunnel."

Urdara leaned forward to look into the hole. "A tunnel to where?"

"I don't know, but it stretches pretty far from what I can tell. It looks like it goes towards Everfall."

"Do you think it's a tunnel connecting the city to whatever this place is?" Teiwa asked.

"Who knows." At'lokias shrugged. He looked around one more time and found a metal ladder behind him. "But it's clearly man-made." He sheathed his sword.

He climbed up the steps and Teiwa offered him a hand as he reached the top. He took it and she pulled him out of the hole but pulled her hand away immediately once he was on ground level. He gave her a confused look, but chose not to question.

"All right," he said, "I guess that's that. Back to our walk, and keep an eye out for any others just in case."

The group continued walking down the main street, careful about their surroundings. Despite their fears, there were no more wraiths nearby. Or at least, none had approached them. It was hard to imagine there would only be one in the entire area if it was in any way connected to Everfall, and all signs indicated to that being the case.

At'lokias walked ahead of them at all times, sword still sheathed. It had proven itself useless against the monster he fought and he had no reason to imagine it would be any different if they ran into more of them.

At last, they reached the outer wall of the small city. Right at the end of the street, the remains of a gate loomed over them and as At'lokias crossed to the other side, Everfall came into view.

However, something else also came into view in the distance.

Dragons.

17

EVERFALL

"We just can't catch a break, can we?" Urdara complained as she joined At'lokias and saw what he was looking at.

Teiwa joined not long after and was just as deflated by the sight.

"Looks like there's only two," At'lokias observed. "So we might be able to get around them. They're huge, though."

The two dragons were much bigger than any At'lokias had ever dealt with, easily larger than even the seafoam dragon that had sunk his family's ship. They sat by what appeared to be the main gate of the city.

"What if we went around them?" Urdara suggested.

"We don't know that there's any other entrances to the city," At'lokias replied, shutting the idea down immediately.

"What if we went back and took that tunnel?" It was Teiwa's turn to try.

"We don't know that it's safe, though." He sighed.

"What do we know, exactly?" Urdara asked, annoyed.

"That there's two huge dragons and we're screwed, basically."

She frowned. It was true, they didn't have enough information to go on and form a plan B. But it wasn't like they could just walk up to the dragons and ask to be let in, either.

"We can get as close as possible without being seen for now, and then wait for them to fall asleep. I doubt they take turns," Teiwa said.

At'lokias' eyes narrowed as he watched the dragons and thought about it. It was most likely their best, if not only, viable option. She was right, it was unlikely the dragons would take turns sleeping, so they only had to be sure they were quiet enough to get past them when they did.

Climbing down to where the creatures sat took a couple hours and by the time they made it down, the sun had risen again and the dragons seemed just as active as they had been at night—which was not much, but still enough that they were an obstacle. Afraid of being seen, the group didn't set up a camp, but rather just sat on the ground to wait.

Hours went by before the first dragon started showing signs of weariness. Once it yawned, the second dragon followed suit and the two curled up and seemingly fell asleep. The trio waited a while still, afraid they might still be awake, before they made their move.

As the three started their slow, silent walk past the reptiles, Teiwa stopped and looked up at one in awe. Up close, it was an even more terrifying sight. With its head on the ground as it slept, the first dragon's eye was taller than they were. It was an enormous beast, its scales a reddish tone and claws shiny in the sunlight. The second dragon was blue, but easily just as large, if not a little more so. They slept close together, but not so close that they blocked the path completely. It was a tight fit, but they could make it if they were careful enough.

As they walked past their snouts, the dragons' hot breath hit them hard enough to almost throw them off balance. They closed their eyes against the heat and when they opened them again, the red dragon's eye was open and looking directly at them.

"Don't move," At'lokias said, hands spread out in a pacifying motion.

Teiwa chanced a look to the side and noticed the dragon had something under its wing. An egg. How had they not seen it this entire time? The dragon followed her gaze and then returned it to her, but still didn't move. The blue one remained asleep.

"Now what?" Urdara asked, still frozen in place.

"I don't think it cares much for us," Teiwa said. "It hasn't moved at all."

"What if we move and it eats us?" Urdara whispered angrily.

"Well, we can't stay here forever either way," At'lokias said and took a tentative step to the side.

The dragon couldn't care less.

He took another step, and then another. When the dragon did nothing, Teiwa followed suit and pushed Urdara into motion. The dragon let out another hot breath and went back to sleep.

"I thought these things were guarding the city," Urdara whispered loudly.

"I guess they know it's just ruins so there's nothing left to guard?" Teiwa said.

"Then why are they here?" Urdara asked.

"I don't know, maybe because it's their home," Teiwa suggested.

"It probably helps that we don't look very threatening to them, too." At'lokias held back a laugh. It seemed a very inappropriate moment for one.

The gate to the city was even taller than the one they'd passed through hours before, and it stood in one piece despite being covered in moss. The inside, on the other hand, was about as run down as the smaller location before had been. The moment they stepped inside, Teiwa stopped.

"This place..." she said, "it feels familiar."

Urdara stopped and looked around. "I'd say you're crazy, but I feel it too."

At'lokias looked at the two and then around as well. "Well, I say you're both crazy, then. I don't feel it."

But Teiwa wasn't listening, her eyes off somewhere in the distance. He called out to her, but she still didn't respond.

"This way," was all she said before she started walking.

Urdara and At'lokias exchanged confused looks before rushing to follow.

Past the initial tall buildings, the city opened into several wide streets. Teiwa walked down a side street with an odd, practiced ease and the two chased after her. As they reached a large two story house, she stopped.

"Here."

"Here what?" At'lokias asked.

"I know this place," she said, "somehow."

Not waiting for them to reply, she walked up to the door and tried it. It opened with a loud creak and she went inside. The other two made various sounds of disbelief and annoyance and walked in after her.

They found her standing in what appeared to be a living room, holding a rug she'd pulled back from the floor. Underneath it, there was a trap door.

"How did you know this was here?" At'lokias asked.

Urdara took a step forward. "This leads to the tunnel we saw back there."

"*How do you* know that?" he asked her.

"I just know, which I imagine is the answer you'll get out of Tei if she stops being weird and actually talks to us."

Teiwa let go of the rug and looked at them. "Me? I don't know, Urdara is right. I just knew it. It's like I've been here before, like I've been here for a long time."

His shoulders deflated and he let out a sigh. Great, both his friends were being weird. And sure, Teiwa had never been the most normal person out there, but this was beyond saving. It wasn't like the plants had told her about the place; that he could accept. But no, she just *knew*. And now they did too, he supposed. As they walked out of the house, he tried to commit to memory exactly where the place was, should they need it later. It was relatively close to the entrance to the city.

"So, do you also just happen to know the way to the tower?" he asked.

"I do, actually," it was Urdara who answered.

"Me too."

"Great," he said.

They walked a little longer before getting back onto the main street. As they walked past houses, they noticed many areas were covered in the same strange goo from before. Urdara led the way, followed by Teiwa and At'lokias at the back. He walked and looked around as he did. Then a strange sight caught his eye.

A wraith. By the window inside a house. He stopped and watched before movement caught his attention. Another one inside a different building. The more he looked, the more of them he found. Most didn't seem to notice him, or at least care, but a few seemed angry and bumped hard against the windows as they tried to reach him. Which was odd, because the wraith he'd fought didn't have a physical form for the most part. Were these different, somehow? One thing seemed certain, however: wraiths didn't know how to open doors.

As he turned to look back to his friends, he noticed they'd moved without him and were quite a ways ahead. He rushed to catch up to them. The main street was blessedly clear of wraiths. He wondered about that, but didn't take much time to think about it, lest he get distracted and fall behind again.

As they reached what appeared to be the main square—there had been a number of squares on the way—a large tower loomed over them.

18
THE TOWER

Everfall's once famous tower was built as a spiral. At its center, there was a pillar that reached from the ground to the top of the building, and the stairs went around it in a circle. On one side of the landings were rooms, used for a variety of things, and on the other were platforms leading to the large pillar. At the very bottom, there was a well deep enough that the water looked nearly black. As the trio stood on the lowest platform and looked down at it, a shiver went down Teiwa's back.

"This place is creepy," Urdara commented, as if she could read her friend's mind. "Let's find this orb and get out of here."

"It's pretty important, so I bet it's on the higher levels," At'lokias added.

"Or maybe that's what they want us to think," Teiwa said. "We should check every room just in case."

"Is that your weird sixth sense talking or your own potentially stupid logic?" Urdara asked.

Teiwa poked her tongue out at her, which served as an answer on its own.

"We might as well make sure," At'lokias said. "It's better than to waste time and energy going up and down this place."

As they argued, a large fin came out of the water. As dark as it was, they could see the silhouette belonging to it. The fish, if that's what it was, was easily larger than a person. As quickly as it emerged, it went back under and disappeared. They took that as a sign to get farther away from the edge.

The first floor lacked a room, with a larger landing for the entrance instead. The second floor's was full of books and papers, spread haphazardly throughout the entirety of the place. Under a large disordered pile, At'lokias thought he saw a skeleton's hand. He didn't linger to confirm.

The tower was reasonably well kept in comparison to the rest of the city. He assumed the people who worked there did their best to try and keep it running for as long as they survived, perhaps in some hope of finding a way of saving them all. Now that he thought about it, there was a remarkable lack of skeletons spread around the streets.

Despite its well conserved state, with few walls falling apart—mostly outside walls in a few rooms, and even then there were only small holes by the windows—the walls were covered in moss and the mysterious goo they'd been seeing everywhere. At'lokias knew better than to touch it.

The floors were so alike that he lost count of how many they'd checked. All rooms had been study rooms, apparently, for they all had papers strewn about and piles of books. He checked those sometimes, but it was always complex and irrelevant to their search.

"What do you think it was like?" Teiwa asked.

"What do I think what was like?" he asked back.

"Being here when it happened. The entire city died. I wonder if it was all at once or slowly. Can you imagine, watching everyone die and not knowing when it will be your turn, just that it will inevitably come?"

"Technically that's just how life in general is," Urdara argued.

"Well, yes," Teiwa conceded, "but faster, right? It must have been terrifying."

"I commend your sympathy for all these dead people we're not running into," Urdara said, "which is weird, if you think about it."

"I was thinking the same," At'lokias said.

"Do you think that's what they used the well for? Maybe they threw everyone down there."

"Gods, Dara, that's morbid." Teiwa shuddered.

"I don't know how deep it is, but I doubt it's deep enough to throw an entire city in," At'lokias argued.

"Maybe that huge fish ate whoever got thrown in there."

"Can we stop?" Teiwa asked. "This is unpleasant."

Urdara rolled her eyes but complied with the request. They continued their search in silence, but no matter how many floors they checked, there still seemed to be more.

As they reached one of the topmost floors, they entered the room to find it surprisingly clean. Though there were many books and papers spread around, they were all organized in neat piles. Atop the table sat what appeared to be a journal. At'lokias approached and took it into his hands.

"Check this out," he called out to the others, "this looks like notes left by the people who worked here."

"And why do we care about that?" Urdara asked.

"It looks like they're about the orb," he replied.

Her interest piqued, Urdara approached him to read the book as well. Teiwa stood by the door when something in the back of her awareness caught her attention. She turned around.

"So, according to this, they did a bunch of experiments on the orb," At'lokias said.

Urdara nodded along. "Looks like they were trying to make the most of it. I don't blame them, but wasn't it entrusted to them for protection?"

"I guess that was a terrible choice." He turned around. "Where's Tei?"

Urdara looked behind her and cursed.

Teiwa stood on the platform, her steps cautious. It was precariously narrow from wear and any wrong step would lead to a fall from who knew how many floors. At the end of it, a crystal was placed atop a pillar, about the perfect size to be held in one's hands. Its inside sparkled and swirled in a pearly white, with occasional colors appearing and disappearing almost as soon as they did. As she approached it, At'lokias and Urdara joined her at the base of the platform.

"What in the world are you doing?" Urdara asked in an angry whisper.

"I found it," was all Teiwa said.

She reached out to it with a piece of fabric in her hand, when something dripped on it. The goo. She looked at it and blinked, then looked up.

A wraith stood on the platform above her, dripping down. It opened its mouth wide and dropped to the platform below. Teiwa screamed and raised her arms to protect herself. It landed between her and the crystal.

At'lokias took a step forward, but another two wraiths dropped down in front of him, oddly liquid-like, and he let out a curse. Behind them, more wraiths came out of the goo on the walls.

"Do something!" Urdara screamed at him.

"On it!" he screamed back, setting the first wraith on fire. Another fell on top of it.

Teiwa took a step back and the wraith in front of her shrieked, limbs writhing about. When it leaned back to pick up impulse and attack, it bumped against the crystal.

It fell from the pillar and teetered on the very edge of the platform. Teiwa lunged under the monster's arms to go after it.

It fell.

She jumped.

19

DIVE

Teiwa fell from the platform head down and reached for the crystal. She managed to catch it and held it close to her chest as she hit the water hard.

"Teiwa!" At'lokias and Urdara screamed in unison.

"She's in the water!" Urdara screamed at him. "We have to do something!"

At'lokias cursed. "Stay behind me."

He made a motion like a circle around them with his arms, creating a large sphere of fire that surrounded them like a shield. The wraiths around them burned with loud shrieks as the two of them bolted for the seemingly infinite stairs. They took them in two steps at a time as more wraiths fell from the ceiling and hit the shield screaming. Urdara ran with her head covered by her arms and shouted whenever another wraith came at them and caught fire.

When they reached the first landing, At'lokias dispelled the shield and rushed to the platform, but Teiwa was already there and he stopped. She lay unconscious on the floor, soaked to the bone and with the crystal embedded in her chest. After a moment of hesitation, he rushed to her side. Urdara was right behind.

"How did she get here?" she asked. "She fell in the water, we saw it."

"Maybe she managed to climb out while we ran down the stairs."

"Have you seen the height of this platform? There's no way she got out without help."

"I don't care how she got out," he barked. "I only care that she did."

He kneeled before Teiwa and put his face close to hers. Urdara watched in anticipation and her shoulders drooped in relief when he smiled.

"She's breathing," he said.

"So what do we do about that?" She pointed to Teiwa's chest. "Pull it out?"

"We can't do that, she might bleed out." He examined the crystal, checking how deep into her chest it'd gone. "She needs a hospital."

At'lokias stood and took Teiwa into his arms.

"Are you serious? You're going to carry her to Stonebrook?" Urdara protested.

"Are *you* going to?" He glared at her. "Besides, I carried you when you collapsed, I can do it with her."

"But that city was much closer to where we were at the time, there's no way you can carry her all the way there!"

"Watch me," was all he said before he stepped out of the platform with Teiwa in his arms.

As they stepped out of the tower, the goo on the walls started to take shape. More wraiths. At'lokias cursed. He wouldn't be able to make another shield while carrying her, and Urdara's magic was cold fire; it wouldn't protect them. But the wraiths didn't know that. He looked at Urdara.

"Can you make a shield for us? I'm kinda busy here."

"But my fire is cold," she said, her voice defeated. "It won't hurt them."

"But it might scare them. Please."

Urdara took a deep breath and copied the motion he'd made, creating a sphere of purple fire around them. The wraiths closest by stood back and she grinned.

"I hate to admit this, but you were right."

"I'm always right." He laughed. "Now let's go."

They walked as fast as they could down the streets, following the inverse route back towards the house they'd visited. It was probably not the most direct way to the main gate, but it was the way they were familiar with. Inside the houses, wraiths by the windows continued to try and charge at them, but failed.

The longer they walked, the more wraiths seemed to become fearless and approached them, but they didn't linger and moved away from them before they could attack.

"It's not working as well anymore," Urdara noted.

"So I've noticed," At'lokias agreed with a grimace.

As they reached the house they'd been in before, they stopped. The street before them was completely taken over by wraiths. At'lokias and Urdara both let out curses.

"Wraiths can't open doors," he said.

"What?"

"They can't open doors, come on!"

He hurried to the door and signaled with his head for her to open it. The two rushed inside and closed it back behind them. She didn't know what good it would do, but she locked it as well.

"Let's take the tunnel," At'lokias said.

"But I thought we didn't know if it's safe," Urdara protested.

"We know the street isn't. Do you see any other way out?"

She grumbled but shook her head. As he continued to carry Teiwa, Urdara pulled back the trap door for him. There was a ladder leading down into it and she went down first. He followed, careful not to shake Teiwa too much or lose his balance.

The tunnel was surprisingly empty and led them back to the other ruins easily enough. Urdara made a fire to help guide their path and so they made it back without further issues. There was no trap door to open on this end, as At'lokias had broken it in his fight with the wraith the day before. Urdara climbed out first and he was right behind, though climbing the ladder with a young woman in his arms was challenging, to say the least.

Going through that alternative path gave them the advantage of avoiding not only the wraiths but also the dragons, which could be in a worse mood now for all they knew, but there was still a long path ahead. Despite that, it was a relatively easy path to follow, the original road still existing, though it was in bad shape.

They traveled day and night with only short pauses, and Teiwa didn't wake at all. At'lokias carried her the entire time, only stopping to rest when Urdara demanded it. His arms and legs burned and he nearly fell from exhaustion multiple times, but refused to stop any more than necessary. They reached Stonebrook by nightfall. As they approached the hospital, Urdara stopped them.

"Wait," she said, "are we just going to walk in there with a crystal stuck in her chest?"

"Why not?"

"Well, what if they won't give it back to us after? Do you want to explain to them what it is and what we need it for?"

At'lokias paused. She was right, there was a chance they'd take the crystal, and then there would need to be lengthy explanations that might not be believed.

"So what do you suggest?" he asked.

"We pull it out now, hide it, and claim she fell on some rocks or something."

He didn't feel particularly fond of the idea of pulling the crystal out, but they were just outside the hospital after all so perhaps it wouldn't be too bad. He took a deep breath.

"Fine," he said, "pull it."

Urdara hesitated for a moment, then sucked in air deeply through her nostrils and pulled. It came out easily. More interesting, however, was there was no sign of a wound anywhere. It was as if it had never been embedded in her chest at all.

The two stared at it for a while. The crystal was perfectly clean, too, not a single drop of blood to be seen. Not knowing what else to do, Urdara shrugged and put it in her bag.

"Let's just say she passed out, then," she suggested.

Once inside, the doctors rushed them into a room and laid Teiwa down on one of the beds. Urdara and At'lokias were made to wait on chairs outside while they examined her. The two were nearly falling asleep when a medic came out of the room to speak to them.

"Your friend appears to be fine," she said. "We can't find any injuries or any reason for this. We'll leave her under observation overnight and see what happens."

At'lokias stood. "May we wait with her? Please."

"I can only let one of you in."

The two exchanged glances.

"You go," Urdara said. "I'll go find us an inn." When he hesitated, she punched him on the arm gently. "It'll be fine, don't worry."

Despite his concerns, the exhaustion was too great and At'lokias couldn't help resting on the chair beside Teiwa's bed. He leaned forward into it and rested his head on his arms and soon sleep had claimed him.

Tired as he was, he'd expected a dreamless night, but was instead haunted by disturbing visions for the entirety of his time unconscious. The wraiths and a pale, lifeless Teiwa created a nightmare like he hadn't had in a while.

Sometime in the middle of the night, Teiwa began to shift in her sleep. The movement was enough to wake At'lokias and he watched her with apprehension. She looked like she was in pain. Before he could call one of the medics to check in on her, she began to scream.

"My eyes! My eyes are burning!"

He stood to call someone but the ruckus was enough that a medic and a nurse rushed in through the door without him needing to. Shining a light into her eyes was too painful for her and they failed to find any explanation for the pain, but a carefully prepared herbal tea soothed her. At'lokias could have died of a heart attack right then, but she seemed fine and he prepared to go back to sleep.

"Loki?" He lifted his head to look at her. Teiwa sat in the bed, wringing the bedsheet. "I'm scared."

"It's all right, I'm right here. Do you want me to hold your hand until you fall asleep?" At'lokias said.

"Can you sleep with me? Like when we were kids?"

He paused. "I don't know…"

"Please."

It hardly seemed appropriate, especially in a single bed, but even in the dark he could see her scared expression. How was he to say no to that? If he woke up early and got out of bed before the hospital staff found them, perhaps it would be fine. He sighed. "All right, make room."

He climbed onto the bed and she moved closer and nestled against his chest. His breath caught and his heart beat so fast he thought it might come out through his mouth. How was he to fall asleep like that? She let out a comfortable sigh and he tried to make himself relax. He forced himself to breathe deeply and wrapped an arm around her.

Sunlight filtered through the curtains and woke him when morning came. He'd barely gotten any sleep at all, with how fast his heart was beating. The moment he climbed onto bed with her and she clung to him, he knew he would spend the night up. It hadn't taken long for her to fall asleep after that, but he worried about waking her, so he stayed by her side. And now morning had come. He watched her, so serene now, and sighed. She shifted again, this time a lot quieter. She started to open her eyes and he smiled.

"There she is. How are you feeling, love?"

"Loki?"

"Everything is all right, we're in Stonebrook. And we have the crystal, so you don't have to worry—"

He stopped.

Her eyes had changed color.

20

CHAOS

"So this is the orb," Ethairadel said as she turned the crystal in her hand. "Though I suppose I can no longer call it that."

At'lokias nodded as he pulled a book out of his bag and flipped through it. "According to these research notes we found at the tower, they cut various pieces off the orb in an attempt to create multiple artifacts, but none of them bore any power. When they concluded it was no use, they simply faceted it so it would look better. Though I'd argue they didn't do that great of a job, it still looks pretty rough."

"That's all very well," Urdara put in, "but does anyone else feel this is kind of cramped?"

The four of them sat on the two beds of the room at the inn, where they were least likely to have strangers listening in on their conversation.

"If you're unhappy, you're welcome to leave," Teiwa said, her arms crossed before her chest.

She'd been in a bad mood for the past two days as they waited for Ethairadel to come and examine her and the no-longer orb, though At'lokias supposed he couldn't blame her for it. Her eyes had not hurt anymore since, but they hadn't returned to their usual color either. Instead of a bright emerald green, they were now aqua colored, somewhere between green and blue.

"She's just in a bad mood because of her eyes." Urdara shrugged.

"We shall get to that," Ethairadel replied, placing the crystal down on the side table. "And how did you determine the crystal was safe to touch with your bare hands after the incident?"

"To be honest, I just forgot about it when I pulled it out of her chest," Urdara said, an awkward laugh escaping her. It sounded completely out of character and left At'lokias disturbed. "Nothing happened though, so we figured it was fine."

"Very scientific," Ethairadel said, a hint of contempt in her voice. "Very well, let us look at your eyes, then." She turned to Teiwa, who sat closer to the edge of her bed for her to look.

Ethairadel waved a hand before her eyes and a light shone on them. She leaned in close to look. "Yes, it appears they have changed colors all the way through. Here, look at the glass of water on the table and do this for me," she said, making a pulling motion with one hand.

Teiwa raised an eyebrow, but did as she was told. Nothing happened.

"Again. Focus on the water."

She squared her shoulders and tried again. This time, the water in the glass moved ever so slightly. Ethairadel hummed in response.

"It is as I thought. The crystal has injected water magic into you."

"The crystal has done *what*?" Teiwa exclaimed.

"Injected water magic into you," Urdara repeated a little louder, but the grin on her face betrayed her desire to mock.

Teiwa glared at her. "This can't be, I'm a sylvan elemental."

"It appears now you have a double affinity, as they call it. Congratulations."

"No," Teiwa said, "don't congratulate me, this isn't a good thing. I'm an aberration. People just don't have two affinities."

"They do, sometimes," Ethairadel said, unconcerned. "It is quite rare, yes. But it does happen. Probably due to similar incidents in past lives, now that I think about it."

"This can't be." Teiwa stood and walked out of the room at a brisk pace. At'lokias apologized to Ethairadel and followed after her.

She ran down the stairs and out of the inn and as she reached the street, she tripped on a root on the ground. Tears weighed on her eyelashes and she couldn't hold them back any longer. He kneeled beside her and pulled her up.

"Hey, it's not that bad, everything will be all right," he said.

She cried harder. He sighed and embraced her.

"I'm a freak!" she screamed. "How is anything going to be all right when I just got another reason for people to treat me like an outsider? I'm never going to fit in anywhere, ever. And I even tripped on a root, I can't even control my own magic anymore! Everything is falling apart."

"That's a bit of an exaggeration," he said, resting his chin atop her head and stroking her hair. "I think you're amazing, and I'm sure there's many others who do too. And I'm sure your magic is fine."

"No, everyone thinks I'm weird, and they're right. And now I even look weird, to boot."

"Nonsense," he pushed her from his arms so he could look at her and wiped a tear from her face. "You don't look weird. You're gorgeous. If anything, I think you're even more beautiful now."

She sniffed. "You say that because you're my friend."

Right, that's why, he thought. "I say it because it's true. Let's go ask Urd, I doubt she will tell you otherwise."

She rubbed one eye with the base of her palm. "You really think that?"

"I really think that. I swear. Now how about we go back? Maybe Aira knows something that can help with your magic, too."

As they walked back into the room, Ethairadel was going through the notes in the book At'lokias had left behind. "There is some truly valuable information here," she said. "You did well to bring this with you."

"I thought it might come in handy," he said.

"They were very thorough. There are instructions on how to use the artifact, as well. You would do well to read this." She held the book up for Teiwa.

"Me?"

"Well, you are the one who will be wielding it, is that not correct? After all, it was you who received the calling."

"Y-yes, I suppose..."

"We have another issue, though," At'lokias put in. "It looks like Tei's grasp on her own magic has been affected."

"Water is her own magic as well, now."

He sighed. "Her grasp on her original magic."

"What makes you think that?" Urdara asked.

"I tripped on a root."

"That's the dumbest thing I've ever heard."

At'lokias glared at Urdara. She mouthed a *what?* at him.

"It is very possible," Ethairadel continued, unfazed by the silent bickering. "Now you have two affinities to handle, so it may be harder to control an individual one."

"Is there anything we can do about that?" Teiwa asked, wringing her hands.

"I suppose... You need a teacher." Ethairadel said. "If you can learn to control your water magic, that should help you find a balance between both affinities."

"That's not important. We need to get the crystal to Yrathea first," Urdara said.

"Au contraire," At'lokias replied, "we can't get the crystal to Yrathea if Tei's magic is a mess. How is she going to use a powerful artifact if she can't even walk around without tripping? We need to get her a teacher first."

The three of them turned to look at Teiwa and she gulped. "I... Uhm... I need some air. Again."

"Actually, I do too," At'lokias said. "Elsewhere."

He stepped out, but rather than leaving the inn after going down the stairs, he turned around and hid underneath them. "I know you can hear me."

"Always," a woman's voice behind him said. "Or rather, most of the time." She chuckled.

He turned around to face her. She looked completely different from the last few times he'd seen her, her skin so pale it reminded him of Ethairadel, and her hair a fiery red that moved around behind her as if she were underwater. Her eyes lacked an iris or a pupil, and she smiled sweetly at him.

"Did you know that was gonna happen to Tei?" he asked.

"I had a vague notion," she admitted. "But I did not know exactly how it would go. In fact, all I know is from your explanation to Ethairadel. I can't see into that city. Still, I think it can come quite in handy, if she can learn to make good use of it."

He hesitated. She never stuck around for long, and he knew he had limited questions before she had to leave again. "Will she be all right?"

The woman looked surprised at the question. "Of course she will, dear. What happened to her is a blessing, though she may not see it this way yet. It will not harm her."

He sighed. "Thank you, Chaos."

Outside, the sun was starting to set and Teiwa wrapped her arms around herself to fight off the chill. At'lokias walked out of the Inn and sat beside her on the bench.

"Are you scared?" he asked.

"Terrified."

"Me too," he admitted. "But everything is going to be just fine. I promise."

"How do you know?"

"I just know," he lied. "But also, as long as we all stick together, I'm sure there's no obstacle we can't overcome." When she stared at him, he laughed. "Too corny?"

The tiniest hint of a smile tugged at her lips. "No, it's fine."

He stood and offered her a hand. "So, what do you say, shall we find you a teacher and take care of that obstacle?"

She looked up at him and took his hand. "Let's go."

-End of Book 1-

Glossary

Teiwa: The protagonist of our story. She's lived in Eastlake her entire life and is only now traveling out of the island. As a Sylvan Tongue, she can speak to plants, though that gift is not well seen among her people.

Urdara: The second protagonist. Teiwa's childhood friend, she moved out of the island when she was a teenager and has since built a thriving business for her family and herself. A fire elemental.

At'lokias: The third protagonist. Childhood friends with Teiwa and Urdara, he left the island when he was fifteen years old without saying a word. What could be behind this? He currently works as a guide for the traveler's guild. A fire elemental.

Ashtari: Teiwa's mother. She always tries to be supportive despite how much she worries about her daughter. Works as a medic at the Eastlake Hospital. A water elemental, her family descends from a foreign people.

Neirrod: Teiwa's father. He is the chief of the island of Eastlake and known to be a kind and fair ruler and a responsible and loving father and husband. A sylvan elemental.

Kadi: Teiwa's younger cousin. She doesn't care for tradition and wants to pave her own path in life. A water elemental.

Numa: Teiwa's aunt. A stay-at-home mother, she's fully dedicated herself to all members of her family. A water elemental.

Balri: Teiwa's older cousin. He works as an island guard, but she thinks he could do much better. A water elemental.

Freyja and Freyj: The twin cousins of Teiwa. Even for children, they're particularly mischievous. Fire elementals.

Trex: Teiwa's former lover who left her in a sudden and insensitive manner. He works as an island guard. A water elemental.

Magic: Everyone in this world possesses a magical affinity with an element. Each person's affinity develops in its own way and some people have abilities others of the same affinity may lack.

Affinities: The elements are air, water, fire, earth, and sylvan. While earth and sylvan may seem the same to an outsider, they are very different, with earth dealing with the actual ground, while sylvan deals with plants.

Seafoam dragon: A type of serpentine dragon that lives in the ocean. Known for guiding ships to safety during storms.

T'rex dragon: A small species of dragon that lives in forests. They are well known for their short arms and for their young's ability to camouflage themselves among plant life.

Guinatee: A species of animal that is often found in cities. Every guinatee is psychically connected to the others, and as such they are often used to send messages to far away locations.

Goldweaving spider: Looks just like a regular spider, but weaves a golden silk. A very rare, very valued species.

Yrathea: The Mother Tree that connects all life in the world. Should something happen to her, the world would be plunged into chaos.

Sacred City: The city of light elves built around and dedicated to defending Yrathea. Its location is a secret to all but those who inhabit it.

Afterword

Thank you for reading Children of Yrathea. This is my first book and I truly hope you've enjoyed it!

I first started this story when I was about fifteen years old, and it's gone through many major changes since then. At the time of publishing, I am currently thirty one years old, so that should tell you something about how long it's been! These characters and this story are very dear to my heart and getting to put them down on paper has been a long time dream of mine, so I am truly grateful that you chose to pick up this book and read it. Thank you, from the bottom of my heart. And if you happen to run into any typographical or formatting errors in this book, let me know! I'll fix it up for whoever picks it up next.

-Amanda

ABOUT THE AUTHOR

Amanda Dimer Silva is an only child and was born and raised in the south of Brazil. She's had a knack for writing stories since a very young age, but only now is getting down to actually putting them on paper. She lives with a very energetic little dog named Meimei.

As a visual arts major, Amanda has worked at the Armazém de Imagens animation studio to produce the movie The Adventures of the Red Airplane. She has also done translation work for several years, and currently edits books. In her free time, she enjoys drawing, reading, playing video games and photographing her ball jointed dolls made to look like her characters.

@amanda.dimers

ALSO BY

BOOKS IN THIS SERIES

- Children of Yrathea (thanks for reading!)

- Saviors of Yrathea (coming soon!)

9 786500 460728